Never Teach a Pig to Sing.

It is a Waste of Time and Besides it Annoys the Pig

Third Edition

By Frieda G Atwood

Published by Kinetic Digital Publishers
www.kineticdigitalpublishers.com
For permissions, inquiries, or other correspondence, please visit our website.
ISBN Paperback: 979-8-90235-051-4
ISBN eBook: 979-8-90235-053-8
LCCN : 2026902825

TABLE OF CONTENTS

Chapter 1

The Scary Nightmare

A child miseducated is a child lost. (John F. Kennedy)

I have come screeching into retirement after a road well-traveled with all the twists and turns, known and unknown, in the world of education. My students were labeled: Regular, Gifted, Learning Disabled, Emotionally Handicapped, Hospital, Home bound or Home Schooled, and they were gathered from all levels of education such as Preschool, Elementary, Junior High, Middle School, High School, Junior College level, committed to Psychiatric Care, and even adult teachers online. I met my students while living and traveling on three continents and one mostly deserted island in the Bahamas.

They taught me every inch of the way through their failures and successes in schoolwork and in developing personalities, as well. I learned so much about student learning that it would be a shame to let their secrets die with me, so I am hoping you will join me as I bring back common sense, the antitheses of the Ivory tower route. It is a welcome breath of fresh air and remember: Teaching is not rocket science.

Let us start off with a quote from Marzano to show you what this the book is not. "For classroom lessons to be truly effective, educators must examine every component of the teaching process with equal resolve. Filled with charts, rubrics and organizers, this methodical, user-friendly guide will help teachers examine and develop their knowledge and skills, so that they achieve a dynamic fusion of art and science that results in exceptional teaching and outstanding achievement." This description was taken from the back flap of the Marzano book "The Art and Science of Teaching" which was selling at that time for $26.95.

How about these questions that I would have generated from reading the quote: What will I do to engage students? What will I do to establish or maintain classroom rules and procedures? And one more: What will I do to recognize and acknowledge adherence to classroom rules and procedures? (From the back flap of the same book.)

It sounds like a scary nightmare. Who would want to go into education after reading just the back flap of the book?

Don't get me wrong. Our education institutions need the Marzanos. The publishing companies need books such as the ones written by Marzano to maintain the status quo of the Ivory Tower.

Montessori was not from the Ivory Tower. She said, "If you are not the person for whom it was intended, it will not reveal itself and it will remain invisible." She was speaking about childhood. This Montessori quote is not as well-known as many of her other quotes. Maybe the reason it is not quoted very often is because it sounds like teachers are born not made. That particular quote has stayed with me for many years. Later, when I finally got to teach the high school level, I learned the same insights were true for this age group of adolescents, as well.

Maybe I can better explain the Montessori quote with this trip to the Keys for a scuba diving trip that I had taken many years ago. After I came up from my first dive, the other divers were gushing about all the sea urchins that were down there and how many they had seen. To hear them exclaiming about the vast amount of life under the water, I was more than amazed. I was perplexed listening to the chatter about sea urchins they saw down there; I was perplexed that I hadn't seen one, not even one. How elusive could they be?

Once it was pointed out to me what to look for, I also saw hundreds of sea urchins myself on my next dive. So, maybe the world of childhood is not quite as elusive as the quote implied. Maybe the magic of childhood can be revealed to you, my reader.

I will not join the ranks of "self- promoting academics, coining buzzwords and aligning themselves on the side of the angels of the moment" but I will avoid "the vague words, fuzzy thoughts or maudlin sentiments that cloud over reality and exercise and have a healthy skepticism toward the kind of fashionable thinking that comes and goes." (Jason L. Riley 2022).

"I believe schools exist for the education of children. Schools do not exist to provide iron clad jobs for teachers, billions of dollars in union dues for teachers' unions, monopolies for educational bureaucracies, a guaranteed market for graduates of teachers' colleges, or a captive audience for indoctrination" (Jason L Riley, 2020) Thank you Jason for articulating so succinctly my thoughts.

So, zip line down from the Ivory Tower and allow yourself to be transformed by the world of students educating their teacher. Take a front row seat and be with me as students revile what is a safe learning environment; work on new productive habits for skill development and tread through the quagmire of politics and just plain evil that exists in education.

Remember that teaching students has been going on since the beginning of time. "The real voyage of discovery is not in seeking new lands, but in seeing with new eyes." (Marcel Proust)

While you are reading all these wondrous and intriguing ideas, remember: you cannot teach a student anything. You can only help him/her to discover it within. (anonymous)

The Mule Gets It

*You can expect more If you inspect more. (**Unknown**)*

She passes the same scene day after day on her way to work. She sees the same scene each time she drives by the farm. A farmer come out of his house, grabs a two by four and smacks the mule between his eyes.

Finally, after witnessing how the same scene plays out again and again, she spontaneously turns into the farm that morning, gets out of her car and walks, rather marches, right up to the farmer.

She asks," Why do you smack that mule every morning in the middle of his forehead."

The farmer said, "Oh, that? That is just to get his attention."

If your student is not in a place to hear you, your words are just noise to be ignored. It is a distraction. Calvin, from the "Calvin and Hobbs" books comes to mind. In one scene, Calvin's class is being told something by the teacher. At the same time Calvin is having one of his daydreams. In the next scene he is in the principal's office and "he come to" and says, "How did I get here?"

While teaching history on the middle school level, I would perform a visual sweep of the class looking for a student who looked like he might be a "Calvin." This is how it plays out. I asked the same question to several students. All the students answer correctly. I ask my "Calvin," the same question, but my "Calvin" answers, "I don't know" with strong confidence - attempting to convey to me, the teacher, that "I don't know" is a real answer. The class laughs. I smile at the class and say, "Wait class, you are going to see real learning take place."

I ask the same question to a couple more students and again ask the same question to my "Calvin" and smile.

He might say, "You already asked that question. "To me he is now actively listening. A light goes on and the student finally answers the question correctly, instead of his "I don't know" answer.

The class laughs and I say, "You just saw learning take place right before your eyes".

A few minutes later, I would ask my "Calvin" student a new question and he would answer the question without hesitation because two other students had already answered the same question correctly. I did not want to risk putting the student back in the same spot, so I gave him an added step for insurance that the tiny step would success. I repeat to the class that they are witnessing real time learning and you the reader are learning as I learned in real time. You are there with me as I developed a good habit of being an active learner in my class. I call it ethical manipulation.

It Cuts like Butter, Your Brain

If I set out to fail but I succeed, did I really succeed in failing?
(Unknown)

I am clarifying the following research because saying what is written today may not be true tomorrow, so I am calling this research 'current brain research' - a list of some of the interesting things we say about the brain.

For example, the brain weighs about three pounds. However, Einstein's brain weighed less than three pounds.

Your brain is always changing. From about six weeks in the embryo until you die, your brain constantly changes connections and grows new cells.

Your brain never stops growing and changing. That means that your lifestyle can help make sure you preserve your mental acuity.

Your brain is 73% water.

There are as many as 10,000 specific types of neurons in the brain.

Events in our brain happen rapidly and are measured in milliseconds.

Once you are familiar with a particular subject, your brain actually reduces blood flow to those areas.

Learning new things helps your brain cells do things more efficiently.

Losing sleep can actually lead to worse memory recall. That is because your brain sorts and stores and dumps the day's information while sleeping.

When you damage portions of your brain, it can re-learn the same tasks in different parts of the brain.

Losing a certain sense can change your behavior in crazy and unpredictable ways. Scientists found that people who suffer from vision loss end up losing weight. Why? Because they couldn't see the food as well!

Long-term memory refers to the brain's ability to store a person's knowledge, skills and experiences. Researchers say if something from short term memory is not re coded within one hour, the information is dumped by the brain.

The researchers found that we produce new neurons in the parts of the brain associated with learning, memory, and emotion throughout life.

The researchers also explain that adopting a more confident and empowered body position can optimize your focus, especially when stress is involved. Teachers in traditional classes 'way back when' were onto something. They were always saying "Sit up straight."

The typical brain comprises about 2% of the body's total weight but uses 20% of its total energy and oxygen intake.

It is estimated that the brain contains roughly 86 billion brain cells.

It isn't until about the age of 25 that the human brain reaches full maturity.

A 2-year-old's brain is 80% adult size.

Brain information travels up to 268 miles per hour.

The average brain generates 48.6 thoughts per minute.

Every minute, 750-1,000 milliliters of blood flows through the brain.

Your brain can process an image that your eyes have seen for as little as 13 milliseconds — less time than it takes for you to blink.

Human brains have gotten significantly smaller over the past 20,000 years.

Your brain can't learn or concentrate on two things at once, but it does switch back and forth between tasks; however, doing so decreases your overall mental performance.

Brain scans clearly show that we use most of our brain most of the time, even when we're sleeping.

Your brain starts slowing down at the ripe old age of 24, but peaks for different cognitive skills at different ages.

Most memory masters will tell you that having an outstanding memory is a skill they developed by employing the best memory techniques.

Research suggests the brains of introverts and extroverts are measurably different. MRIs reveal that the dopamine reward network is more active in the brains of extroverts while introverts' brains have more gray matter.

You may remember the emails that came out showing words with mixed up letters. The order of letters in a written word doesn't matter much to your brain. If the first and last letters are in the right spot, your brain can rearrange the letters to form words as fast as you can read.

The latest research shows that the brain's memory capacity is in the petabyte range. A petabyte is a quadrillion, or 1015 bytes.

The human brain is capable of 1016 processes per second, which makes it far more powerful than any existing computer.

Memories are shockingly unreliable and change over time.

Emotions, motivation, cues, context, and frequency of use can all affect how accurately we remember something.

Of the thousands of thoughts, a person has every day, it's estimated that 70% of this mental chatter is negative, self-critical, pessimistic, and fearful.

Ninety-five percent of your decisions take place in your subconscious mind. (I can't get my head around that concept.)

The Wongs Got It Wrong

The test of a good novel is dreading to begin the last chapter.
(Unknown)

Harry and Rosemary Wong wrote "The First Days of School." "If I had had to read it, before starting teaching, I would have run away fast, very fast; but as a reference for a teacher, there are parts that I found useful.

The quotes were good, and the topics were abundant. The book, as other books do, tell you what to do. There is "so" much to do. The book points out effective versus ineffective but how do you replicate effective; and how do you know you are being ineffective? How does a teacher get from point A to point B. What are the steps to get from point A to point B? What is the easiest path? Is it possible? Why do you want to go in the first place?

For example: You want the students to stay in their seats until given permission to leave the seat. A student gets out of his seat. Is this cause for punishment? No! Point A begins with the explanation of the procedure and routine.

Each procedure is always based on the premise for the safety of the student. The parents expect the teacher to keep their child safe.

The final step the students showed me is usually glossed over, as well. Practice. Practice. Practice. A clue that the practice period is going well is when you hear a student pointing out to other students the correct procedure or routine that you as the teacher insisted the students follow.

Once you have stated the procedure or routine, given the logical reason and students have accepted the procedure or routine through successful practicing, you are on your way to establishing a safe, logical, mutual classroom management system in which the teacher picked up the students at point A, and then moved them to point B. Point B makes for an enjoyable class to look forward to each day. Ethical manipulation.

Hierarchy of Needs

*If I bought the worst of the Beetles, and I liked it, should I ask to get back my money? (**Unknown**)*

Wong defines allocated time as 100%; instructional time as 90%; engaged time as 75% and learning time as 35%. (Wong) What does that mean? Run away and run fast.

Practice time in class is overlooked and can be the best part of any class on any grade level. Students learn the skill, practice the skill and get tested. How about making more use of 'practice, practice, practice' as a whole group activity? There is a word for that. It is called a game.

It can be a game played alone or with a partner or even teams. I have had 'half-class' teams made up where one half of the class goes against the other. I have had kids go individually against the clock for the fastest time.

My favorite type of practice session which the students taught me, is called "checkout students." For example: The class is learning the meaning of the assigned prefixes for the day - about 7 to 10 at a time. When a student thinks he/she is ready to demonstrate mastery, I check out the student by asking the meaning of the assigned prefixes. Once the student has been checked out by me, I assign the student as 'checkout student'.

The practice session is over when all the checkout students are now looking for a student to check and there are none because everyone earned checkout status. It can create a cacophony, but I listen for prefix chatter and end the practice session before the students cross over to social chitchat. Ethical manipulation.

The Power of Sincere Praise

Everyone has potential. You just need to know where they are coming from and meet them there.

Research indicates that praise used optimally can result in learning. The praise should be varied, specific, given quietly and with great feeling. Effective praise attributes the student's success to effort and ability, expecting success in the future. Effective teachers use 6 specific praise or encouragement statements per 50-minute period. I will expand this concept to include effective praise for individual students. Sprinkle the necessary correcting with compliments. Five positives to one negative. (Some say four and some say three.) The point is that if you have just given a student two negatives in a row, you have a problem brewing. Deal with it soon in a common-sense way.

Use a lopsided ratio and you will hear "Stop picking on him" from other students. Use the correct ratio and your student will accept criticism and believe you like him/her while you are calling out the student.

Let's stop there and make one important correction at this point. Let's change the vocabulary for this topic. Use the word 'feedback' instead of effective praise and criticism. Feedback is constant and continuous. Think of a practice session in a sport like football practice. I am sure many examples come to mind.

For a school example: On the first day of class say, "You came into the room quietly, class." "I like it when you can come in quietly and get to work." "Coming in quietly is greatly appreciated." The next day, you might put out a reminder. "Class, remember to come in quietly like you did yesterday." "You all did a good job yesterday." "That was a good entrance today. Let's try for three days in a row." "Yesterday was your best job." Remember, it takes 21 days to learn a new habit and most people give up on day 17.

While the students are coming in quietly and going about their work, I can take attendance. Perhaps you did not know that school attendance is a legal document in a court of law, so I need to get it right.

The rule simply becomes the procedure that everyone is practicing for a real reason. Another logical reason is safety. You can point out that their parents expect me to keep them safe, which is true. I don't want anyone to get pushed, shoved or trampled. If one of them got hurt, their parents would want to know why I'd let them come into the room pushing and shoving.

As most of the students buy into the entrance procedure and use the procedure to gather self-esteem, it is time to single out one of the students who is not consistently buying into the procedure and, for example: Say "Tom, go out and come in quietly as the rest of the class was able to do."

At this point you now have only the outliers to provide negative feedback, offering them a chance to correct themselves, while complimenting the whole class (which is the usual way or process when establishing a new procedure). The outliers will get better at the procedure of entering the room. These students need more practice and will appreciate your consistency. When you hear students telling other students how to come into the class, it is time to move on to a new procedure. This one is accepted and practiced.

If you apply Maslow's theory to this 'entering the room procedure', the student is taken through the hierarchy of needs. Maslow's theory states that "humans are motivated to fulfill their needs in a hierarchical order". His theory begins with the most basic needs before moving on to more advanced needs.

Maslow pointed out that the first needs of a student are: physiological needs - food, clothing, shelter, safety and security, i.e. The need to feel free of physical danger or danger of being denied ways to meet basic physiological needs. Maslow said the highest need is self-reliance and Montessori said that the highest need for her students was working as though she was not there. A great leader allows the followers to believe they did it themselves.

Successful mastery of the 'entering the room procedure' also satisfies the social, or 'affiliation' need for acceptance and approval from peers and helps increase dignity prestige and self-esteem, (i.e., the need to be recognized and valued by others), Finally, the outcome of self-actualization, which is the need to fulfill one's potential or do what one believes is important from one's own point of view, is achieved.

Students taught me to design the rules as class procedures and take the students through Maslow's hierarchy of needs while practicing the class procedure - whether it be sharpening a pencil or passing in papers. Ethical manipulation.

Habits – Good and Bad

Consider the postage stamp: Its usefulness consists in the ability to stick to one thing till it gets there. **(Joseph Billings)**

Later I started teaching students along with the 'material'. Ability is what you are capable of doing. Attitude determines how well you do it. (L Holtz) Let's expand this concept. Holtz made a good start using the word "ability". Bring into the classroom as many abilities as you can draw out of the students - from skateboarding to gymnastics. – in school and out. Mismatch is when you wonder why a kid can excel at football but not write an essay. There is no pattern to acquiring abilities. Abilities are better understood in terms of as many small habits as possible. It takes a lot of habits to develop an ability. Some habits are good and some distasteful - like picking your noise in public. Some habits are useless. Some are destructive, such as addiction to drugs.

Find an ability of a student and use it to your advantage in class. Try ways to move the helpful habits to the problem area in the learning process and apply, adjust and practice. "It takes twenty-one days to learn a new habit and most people quit on day 17".

An example: While teaching at Andros Island in the Bahamas I heard a success story. Allen asked Elena to write the labels for his picture because she is good at writing; and I heard Elena ask him to draw a whale for her because he draws so well. I heard this from my two former bickering students who had not previously considered each other's strengths and weaknesses, good habits and bad.

Chapter 2

The Power of Sandra's Belief System

Oh, the difference between nearly right and exactly right. (Unknown)

While teaching at Garrison School in Dover, N. H. I gave out the first weekly spelling assignment and Sandy sat there crying quietly. When I asked what was wrong, another student said, "She only gets 10 words a week instead of 20 words."

Well, as a new teacher in my new year assignment, I needed to find out about this apprehensive girl. I said "That's OK. We will teach you to learn 20 words a week." I wondered why I said that being a poor speller myself. I had no way to fix my spelling problem. What could I do for her?

I later learned she lived on her family farm not far from the school. She had her own horse and was quite good at riding. Sandra was pretty and was well liked by her peers. They were protective of her, as well.

I got a volunteer as her spelling partner; one of her friends, and she learned 20 words for the first spelling test. She must have received 100 because we used the same system all year. That was my best plan because I couldn't spell myself.

The school subscribed to one of the paperback book orders magazines, like Weekly Reader or Scholastic Magazine. Each month I put a student in charge of counting the money for the order. Sandra was in charge for one week and she picked two friends to help her.

They stayed in at recess to count the money and get the order ready for me. Real life math, right? They took more than the usual one recess to get the order ready for me. I never knew if she and her friends needed the time or were having too much fun together.

Next year, I heard from a guidance counselor from the Junior High that Sandra subsequently attended, that she went to that guidance counselor on her own and asked to get out of the "dumb classes" and she did.

Cuisenaire Rods are Lightning Rods for Math

Lost dog Three legs, Broken tail, Right ear missing, Accidentally neutered, answers to the name, Lucky.

Cuisenaire Rods are a versatile collection of rectangular rods of 10 colors, each color corresponding to a different length. They provide endless opportunities to introduce, investigate, and reinforce key math topics such as addition, subtraction, geometry, measurement, multiplication, and division.

Students who are having problems learning the addition tables are probably 'whole picture' students rather than students who can normally rote memorize the tables. The rods explain the big picture.

For example: The rote memory ability student is called 'field independent'. The field independent mind can look at a puzzle already in pieces and can put the puzzle together piece by piece without any concerns about what it should look like.

The opposite is the 'big picture' student who needs to know the whole big picture to make sense of the parts. 'Big picture' students are also called 'field dependent'. A field dependent mind needs to know "what's it all about?". This type of mind likes to know how the parts fit together. This type of mind needs the picture on the puzzle box out in front while working. Cuisenaire rods demonstrate the whole picture and were invented for the big picture mind.

Instead of the rods, you can show the relation of numbers with a strip of paper divided up in ten equal parts. Bend over the first two squares and ask how many squares are needed to get to ten. Fold the strip in half and demonstrate five plus five is ten.

Give the paper strip to the student to put in his/her pocket for further use, hopefully at home. When a parent asks that age old question "What did you learn in school?" The student reaches in his pocket and pulls out the number strip and explains how it works and what it shows. This is an example of Montessori and Confucius logic. I say common sense.

Put 10 strips of paper together to show the relationship of ten tens=100, etc. Sell the students the concept of patterns. There are many patterns in nature and school learning, as well.

Julius Caesar Dies but Saves the Class

"We are what we repeatedly do.

Excellence, therefore, is not an Accident. It is a habit". (Unknown)

Our elementary reading teacher, Donna, lent me the book during my second year's teaching. I was teaching at Garrison school in Dover, New Hampshire. The book was called, "Push Back the Desks" by Albert Cullum, published in 1967 by Citation press. What? She just gave me permission to push back the desks and have fun? Do I dare? It was only my second year as a teacher.

Cullum had rewritten "The Julius Caesar" keeping in the famous lines but also writing great lines for the throng (or crowd) scenes. I got Julius Caesar 'ditto copied' so everyone got a copy. I chose my lower-level readers because they needed experience. We went on a school field trip to the Library at the University of New Hampshire because we knew nothing about Julius Caesar and the students looked forward to getting out of school and riding the big yellow bus.

We brought back any book that depicted the Roman era. We wanted to know what they looked like, when and where they lived in the world, what kind of clothes they wore, and who was Caesar, anyway? In the end, the students turned a white sheet from home into a Roman robe, put it over their clothes, and wore sandals if they had them. They picked flowers for their garland and put on a performance for the whole school.

The hardest part for the students was accepting the reality of learning their lines. During the performance we had several scenes, so I managed backstage and never got to see the actual performance; but I did see their happy faces, dripping smiles all over each other after exiting the stage and coming back into our little off-stage area. They were a hit!

I got to teach summer school that year because Donna oversaw the summer school program. It was a coveted job because you made teacher pay, but with reduced hours and small, small classes. Summer school is where I dared to direct Albert Cullum's other play about a circus. In his circus, students played with the trainers, the animals and the ringleader. We performed for the rest of the students in summer school. Of course, I hoped it hooked some kids on reading because the summer reading program was far from remedial. I didn't get to teach summer school for another 20 years. That's a great story, too, and it starts now.

It was at Madison Middle school. By now I was certified in reading, so I got to teach summer school to the students who were in danger of failing their regular class. In their foolish wisdom, the educators made the students who were in danger of failing take a virtual class online at home. The students who were not motivated in the regular class were even less motivated to work online; so that is where I came in. I am not making this up. The students remained in the virtual class with their virtual teacher. My job was to make the uninterested students call their virtual teacher from the phone on my desk when there was a problem or question about the assignment. My other task was to tell the students to keep working online at their computer, provided for them for their virtual class.

Breakfast and lunch were also provided to each student free of charge. The students managed to leave so much of the healthy food uneaten that it took two maintenance employees to cart off each of the large trash barrels that were provided for the after-meal trash.

All my 15 students - really 15 students - passed their virtual class because my taskmaster assignment meant I was effectively an individual coach for each student. I would help each student trouble-shoot their problem, formulate the questions for the virtual teacher and have each student call the virtual teacher. I would then have the student explain to me what the virtual teacher had said. I stuck to my role as coach, knowing it would be quicker and easier to help the students myself. Unfortunately, I was cut, but re-hired the following year, so I missed out on teaching summer school the following year.

Bully

*Bullies don't have happy birthday parties. **(Unknown)***

During my second-year teaching at Garrison in Dover, NH, a boy in my class was reported to me by another student. Today, it would be called bullying. The two girls came to me and said George was calling them names. Without hesitating I said "Call him a name. A name he does not know". I came up with Lake Titicaca which is a lake in Bolivia, the largest lake, and we would be learning about that lake in coming weeks. There was nothing bad about the word. It was just unknown and confused the bully. For good measure I may have thrown in that the girls were to laugh after saying Lake Titicaca and walk off. The tables were turned. The bully now provided them with a sense of amusement instead of dread. The girls had their ammunition and went laughing off to recess. It worked like a charm and that was the end of the bully story. Work smart, not hard.

While teaching at the Alternative School, I used a more direct approach. The time between classes was three minutes. You wouldn't think there would be bullying between classes. Lydia was a large teenage girl who came into my class yelling, "Leave me alone."

I asked her who was bothering her. Of course, she said "no one", so I went into the hall and told the usual group of boys that they were to leave her alone and that she had a right to a peaceful day without any of them ruining it between classes. Every day I stood guard, letting the boys know I was serious about them, leaving her alone. I could only guess what she had been putting up with from them. She never said, "thank you", but I did get a smile from her when I asked how her day was going; because I did check in with her daily at first and then sporadically throughout the weeks. Her home life was not easy, but at least she could count on a peaceful school day.

Between the beginning of my career and the end, I would spot possible bully victims and help them assimilate into the class without having to deal with being a victim.

One year while teaching at the Middle School level, my student, Tony, took over the role of protector. Eric's sneakers were put in the toilet one day in PE class. From that day on, Tony included Eric in his group and even ate with him and his group.

I was Indoctrinated in the Second Grade

*"Don't mind criticism. If it's untrue, disregard it. If it's unfair, keep from irritation. if it's ignorant, smile. if it is justified, learn from it." **(Unknown)***

I decided to become a teacher while in the second grade. My teacher's name was Mrs. Battles. She spoke with a smile all day long, day after day. When you ask students about a teacher that the student liked, the first remark is, "She was nice." The smile must have meant she was nice, but she was more than nice. She made us work. We were always busy.

This was also the age of the teacher's little desk bell. It was the same bell you would ring at the hotel desk to call the bell man. It was a great plan for procedures and routines. She rang the bell in a way to give you a clue about how mad she was, pretend mad.

I remember the bell mostly from reading seat work time when I was in school. It was a traditional classroom environment. One ding meant "settle down, I still have my smile"; but when we heard her 'mashing' the bell, we knew that we, the students, had gone too far and we would even stop our feet from shuffling under our desks. In a short time, we would ease up and relax.

Mrs. Battles did her own art in those days, and I fell in love with the smell of finger paint and how freely my fingers were able to make marks. One time we did the 'Chicken Little' story. I got to draw and paint Turkey Lurkey with finger paint Look up the story and see how magnificent my Turkey Lurkey must have looked.

Later on, jumping ahead in time, I discovered tempera paint. I thought it was more acceptable than finger paint and I scrounged a great deal of the coveted tempera paint from Melanie, the art teacher at Garrison School. We made a lot of maps on my three bulletin boards for social studies classes. We worked hard and had fun, too. Hmmm, where did I pick up that theory? Out of nostalgia, I wanted to use a bell, but it was perceived as old fashioned, so instead, I said "Too noisy. Go back to your seats and we will try again." In those days my students could draw and paint and write on the bulletin boards in groups while whispering every word and not spilling the precious tempera paint.

During my second-grade experience with Mrs. Battles, Christmas parties were a big deal. We could bring a guest for the day. What was Mrs. Battles thinking? I had my younger brother come to school with me for the day of the party. We just had to bring a gift for our company. My mother would buy a set of all the types of life saviors.

Each kind was in a roll and fitted into a book-like box case. When you opened the case, there were rows and rows of life saviors. To me it was all the candy in the world. I felt sorry to give it away as a gift at the Christmas party. The whole set cost 50 cents. We had none of those cases of life saviors at home.

Because phonics was a big part of the reading program, I remember being embarrassed that my teacher saw how bad I was at it – red X marks all over my phonic workbook pages while my understanding of the material remained fine.

I looked forward to the wildflower contest she held each spring. My brother won it the year before, so I expected to win this year because we both had my grandmother as our guide. I won the contest. The reward was a simple shout out from the teacher in front of the whole class. Back then we didn't know about trophies and ribbons for participation.

At the end of the year, Mrs. Battles had me take home a schoolbook to read over the summer, as though that would help fix my reading problem. The name of the book was "Blacky the Crow".

On thinking back, I felt liked by Mrs. Battles. I never wanted to be one of the 'bad' students. We only had one. She used routines and procedures effortlessly. Hmmm, that is where I learned to make each student feel special because I knew what it felt like. I remember a student saying in the early years, "You like all the students, but you like some more."

Get the Dynamite Out of Your Class

Sometimes you have to exaggerate things in order to get people to see the truth. ***(Unknown)***

Long gone are the days you command respect because of your title; but you still have an ace up your sleeve. You get only one absolute in teaching. Use it often and creatively and never give it away. Don't give up control of the seating plan. about the seating chart and desk arrangement.

The most severe use of the seating chart was a high school teacher I knew who put a number on every desk. You stood and waited to be called in alphabetical order for your seat assignment. Instantly, his new students knew not to ask this teacher a question and they were sure he was going to be strict.

In a kinder gentler world, the elementary teacher put a name tag on your desk. When you had a seat change, you took your whole desk.

Of course, on the other hand, there is no seating chart. I am not referring to the 'seminar type' class or 'sit around the table' class. Even with no seating chart, as in college, students make use of part of the herd mentality to sit in the same seat, class after class; so a seating chart on that level becomes a moot point.

The well-used seating chart is up there with the Queen's staff. You command where even the toughest student's bottom will sit and for how long. Kids just don't go against the seating chart. It is well marshaled by peers, too.

A spontaneous seating chart adjustment in the middle of the class lesson may be good for your self-esteem. Talkers - Had enough of the talkers? - put one next to a non-talker. Power Groups - Break up small, powerful, popular groups (the in-crowd) and pair a popular student with one of the 'out crowd'. Isolation - A student who needs isolation: move to the first seat in the row by the window (but not the back of the room). That is where we put 'those students' in the days of old. Scrapper students - You will sit together on one condition. You two will sit together until you are friends. An annoying habit; e.g. a student who is constantly using the chair in front of him to keep his big feet entertained. Put him in the front row with no chair in front of him. Individualism - I had one student who made an office for himself in my class. He would set up his office each period and put it away at the end of class.

Carol, the fourth-grade teacher at Frankfurt International School (FIS) used the first seat in the row as a help station. She would select different students from time to time to command the first seat in the row. If you had a question, you had permission to get up and walk to the student at the help station in your row.

After a winter break, the floors would be polished and the kids would come into a class with a new desk configuration and of course, a new seating plan. The teacher gets to have another first day. The power of the seating chart is still in the teacher's hands.

One time while teaching at the Alternative school, several new students entered the program at one time. Instead of going to their assigned seats they changed seats. During attendance taking, I had to send students back to their assigned seat. Unfortunately, my phone butt dialed my son who so enjoyed listening to me getting the students back in the seats according to MY seating chart. The mutiny from the new students was aborted and my son got a few laughs.

Feedback is a Mighty Catalyst

Those who thwart our best efforts, whose psychological needs are such that our classroom became a stage for acting out their own demons.
(Unknown)

While at Garrison School, in the days of teaching material rather than teaching students, I gave lots of grades because I wanted students to know how they were doing and how I was doing, as well. I called it "the importance of feedback". If the students were getting good grades, then I was doing well, too. The teacher was linked to the success of the students. I was as good as they were, scoring on class tests and the yearly standardized tests. Feedback on grades was my way of bridging the gap between teaching students rather just teaching the curriculum.

My observation was this. Whether the students received many grades or, on occasion, fewer grades, the results were the same. Students generally averaged the same from one marking period to the next. The 'A' student remained an 'A' student and the average student remained average.

I learned of the Bell Curve, and that threw off my thinking. According to the Bell Curve, I should have had as many 'F' students as 'A' students, as many 'B's as 'D's, with the majority receiving 'C' average, hence the Bell Curve. But if the Bell Curve was heavy with 'A's, then I was an easy grader. On the other hand, if I had the majority of students receiving a 'C' grade, I was successful, according to the Bell curve; but to me, I was an average teacher because the majority of students were in the 'C' category. I did not believe I was an easy teacher. I generalized that I set what is now called 'the rubric' for my students; but I taught them how to achieve more than they expected of themselves. The students in turn expected more of themselves; so, the upward spiral was established as normal. The more I adjusted and arranged the input the students received from the feedback from tests and myself, the better they performed.

Later when I started teaching high school students, I gave better feedback to the students by changing my grading system. This was my plan. I gave out weekly averages. Not only did I average each week for each student, but I used a different system. For example: A = 4 points, B = 3 points, C= 2 points, D 1 point and 0 points for an F. If a student had 90, 75 and 82 for weekly grades, the numbers would be 4+2+3 = 9/3 = 3 which was a 'B' average.

A marking period would be emphasized in weekly averages rather than waiting the traditional six weeks for feedback to be given to the student on a report card.

For example: An 'A' average from last week would be averaged with a 'C' average for the current week; so the current grade for the grading period is now a 'B'.

With this method, students always knew where they stood on a weekly basis, and it gave the students a plan for the next week. It was my way to give more control and responsibility for their grade back to the students. It was their grade, really, not mine. Too many students at the secondary level left the grade to chance or even did not bother with their grade. By now, at this level, too many accepted their ranking as a 'D' or 'F' student. "That's what I always got, and I passed." said more than one low achieving student.

But now it was the age of state testing and the students had to pass the state testing to graduate. The other part of my plan was to teach students how to take a reading test and pass the state test. To do that, I taught the vocabulary of the test such as the 'main idea' and how to figure where to look for clues and pick the right answer for the main idea question. For example: 'Main idea' was an easy concept but which of the similar answers was correct? I had my students practice where to look for the main idea: title, first sentence, last sentence and any pictures. The differences in the choices for answers became obvious; rather than the choices all sounding similar, which had previously led them to simply guess "eeny, meeny, miney, moe". The best part was that no one had read the story yet.

The first habit I taught was to have the students read all the questions first. With the questions read first, the brain would be looking for the answers as they read. It is called 'reading for purpose'. Using this method with my at-risk students in my first year at Titusville High, the Florida Curriculum Assessment Test (FCAT) - showed an increase of 7 percentage points at the high school level.

Dr. Christy hired me for the position of reading teacher. Like minds converged. He agreed that my students could read. I had never found a non-reader in my remedial classes. Mostly, they did not like to read, and they were clueless how to take a state test in reading. There was just too much reading on the reading test for many of the students to care enough to put in the effort.

At Quest elementary school in Brevard County, I had my own reading group - even though I was a resource teacher for the whole grade/school. Margret, a seasoned teacher, gave me her 'at risk students' who were at risk of not getting a 300 on the Florida Curriculum Assessment Test. (FCAT) If a score of 300 was not gotten, the county mandated the student to stay another year in grade three. No pressure!

One student was deaf in one ear; one was not interested in academics or reading in general - let alone the Fl state-mandated test. Another was a 'learning-disabled gifted' student who refused help. One student was a sight reader with a poor grasp of phonics, and one was labeled at that time, a slow learner. Learning was slow going with a great deal of repetition.

This is the plan revealed to me by the students and the plan went like this. For my non-academic student we used his goal, which was to see his father in the summer. He was not going to see his dad in the summer if he did not pass the state-mandated test. For my non-phonics student, I taught her to sound out words by syllables so that she did not need to pronounce each word correctly to understand the story or answer questions about the story. She lightened up and was easier on herself. She bought into my plan because it sounded easier than reading the story and answering the questions. My deaf student was going to pass to the next grade anyway, because of her disability. My student who did not want help took in my new habits from a distance. My little ragtag group made me proud; they all passed the state testing and were promoted. My deaf student missed the cut off by two points but would pass. My sight reader (slow learner) outscored them all. My non- academic student kept his trip to see his dad in the summer. I admit to overusing his goal to keep him serious and motivated. My learning-disabled gifted student smiled at me. He said, "told you I would pass." He must have been listening.

The secret to my plan was constant feedback on how they were doing with whatever new habit I had them practice.

I used the same approach to my social studies class on the middle grade level at Madison Middle School. From previous test results, we practiced how to pull out all the reasons from the paragraph which would be needed for the mandated writing test. We read the questions first, learned the vocabulary of the test and practiced where to look for the answers. I was so proud of my students for buying in to my plan and me for planning it.

Unfortunately, I was called to a surprise meeting. In the meeting, I got instant feedback. My team disagreed with my plan. The English teachers, along with the rest of the team, were there and the reading coach was there, as well as the principal. The students had told the English teachers they didn't have to read the story first. The English teachers were outraged that I had told the students this.

The reading coach had a state-mandated practice test with her, so I demonstrated how to find the main idea without reading the story.

Impressed, they were not. How dare I tell students not to read the story. No kudos for me. No "lets learn from her plan" either.

After I demonstrated how to find the main idea, the principal said, without any discussion with any of the teachers, "Please do not tell them they don't have to read the story." The meeting was over.

Test results showed I had 29 students who earned 5s on the reading test. A five was the highest grade on the state-mandated test. I taught reading comprehension through my social studies classes with constant feedback to the students on how they were doing with learning the skills. They took their learned skills to the FCAT reading and writing test as well. The skills worked together for the reading and writing test and there were even more numerous writing scores that were 5s, too.

I got cut at the end of my second year. Last one hired and the first one to be cut.

Glad I took an Acting Class in College

*"Every day of my life I'm forced to add another name To the list of people who piss me off". (**Unknown**)*

My first student-teaching assignment was in a third-grade class in a white suburban neighborhood. During my nine weeks I was put through the paces. I learned to plan out every detail of my lesson plan starting with a hook to capture the students' attention. After every lesson, Louise, my supervising teacher, would go over every detail of my presentation, pointing out what went on as well as anything that needed to be fine-tuned in my next lesson plan. It was during this time I realized each lesson was a performance and I was the star of my own show.

In the future, I critiqued my day, every day on the ride home, pointing out to myself what went well and what needed to be fine-tuned.

It was during my first-year teaching sixth graders at Garrison School that I noticed I was teaching students as well as the curriculum in my lesson plans. More astounding was the realization I was putting on a live performance every day, five days a week, week after week, for

180 days a year and the variables affecting my well-planned lesson were the students.

It was students like Sandra at the beginning of this chapter who were an eye opener, my epiphany. Now, not only did I have to create winning lesson plans to be accountable to the curriculum, but I also had to find ways to make sure each student was learning. This began my quest to pay attention to how each student learns and match them up with the next step necessary in the process of learning a skill to mastery level. I began using the Bell Curve on every test and put the results on the board. I explained that my new goal would be to move my 'D' and 'F' students up to 'C', 'B' or 'A'. I also said if the class got all 'A's and 'B's, "they" would say the teacher was too easy and not challenging students, but I would be proud of them.

I also paid attention to Glasser who said, "Students remember 10% of what we read, 20% of what we hear, 30% of what we see, 50% of what we both hear and see, 70% of what is discussed, 80% of what we experience personally and 95% of what we teach to someone else." (William Glasser)

Practice took on a new meaning. I could not go home with students for homework hour, so I taught the students how to build a homework plan and take care of the plan.

This was the winning plan for homework. Decide where you can study and do homework. Get permission. Decide who will help you at home (If you fight with your sister, don't pick her). Decide on the time. Some students get on it right away, some get to it after a snack, some work while dinner is being cooked, some after dinner. For the many students who have outside activities, the homework is often done on the bus ride home.

The important part of the plan is that it accounts for all the family activities for each day and each and every family member knows the plan for the week. Post your homework plan in your notebook or even on the refrigerator. With an adult the plan is tweaked weekly depending on the family activities. Commit and hold yourself accountable. "It takes 21 days to learn a new habit and most give up on day 17."

Politics at Garrison School

"Life is what happens to yourself While you are making other plans." (Unknown)

I knew nothing of the word politics when I started teaching. Note to self. Add politics in education class to the curriculum for future teachers. I got my introduction at Garrison School - my second school assignment.

Sitting there with my principal was the assistant superintendent of the schools. Great, I thought. The Assistant Superintendent must have heard of me starting the safety patrol program, being the coach for girls' basketball, being an active participant in improving the Parent Teacher Association and of course my amazing teaching skills.

When I heard the first negative from Mr. Rivers, the principal, I interrupted him to remind Mr. Rivers that he never came to my room the whole year and that I had had only one meeting with him all year. The rest of the evaluation faded, and I got to come back the second year. Silly me, I thought I had politics figured out even though I had still not learned the real meaning of the word. Just tell the truth and good wins over evil, right?

Mr. C. I. Blaine

Be kind. Everyone is fighting a battle. **(Unknown)**

I got married and went with my new husband to the SAC Base in Goldsboro, North Carolina after graduating from college. During my first job interview, I was asked if I had a problem with Negros. I said I only knew one from my high school years. Her name was Dolly White (really). There was one Negro at my college, and he played soccer on the school team, but I did not know him. I said "no" and found myself as the first white teacher in School Street School. I was there when Martin Luther King marched through on his way to Washington, D.C.

I came from farm country in rural New Hampshire. What did I know about anything? At my new school, called School Street School, not one teacher mentioned I was white, and I did not mention they were black. I did not know there was a Freedom March on its way to DC, either.

However, the principal, Mr. C. I. Blaine, spoke race with me when I was in his office. He said he and his wife were living in the white world. but never said the word white. He enjoyed it, but his wife, his first-grade teacher, wanted to come back to her people - so they did.

I was an observer. I watched students play on the broken glass covered playground and did not get cut. I monitored lunch daily by eating with my class. I learned the words 'chitlin' and 'collard greens'. Blacks did have a collective smell. It came from the food they ate. The Viet Cong used to find the Americans in the jungle from their smell, which came from the American diet - especially the meat.

I let the students in early on those frosty mornings because they were not dressed for the cold. In science, I taught about how a furnace, which none of them had, worked in a house. It was a new science book, too.

Julia used to come up to my desk and softly touch my hair. She liked to run my hair through her fingers. (I had long blond hair.) The students and I didn't talk about race, either.

I left and scurried home to the farm when my husband was deployed to Korea during the USS Pueblo Crises.

This was my first teaching assignment, and I didn't last the year. I went back to visit the class and Mr. C.I. Blaine. I learned Julia got moved to the other second-grade teacher because she bit the new teacher. The second-grade teacher next door kept a stick at her desk.

It was years later when I met my Florida Blacks at Memorial Middle School after returning from teaching in Germany. They were not called Negros anymore. They were trying to learn how to rap and thought it was cool to enter a room spewing their rap beats. (No words, yet.)

A few years later, I met my Blacks again at THS. They were calling me a racist. Where was the woman who kept a switch at her desk? Actually, one Black teacher at Memorial Middle did really keep a switch at his desk made from a broken fishing pole. The family unit was still breaking down.

I mentioned this teaching assignment because there were no school politics involved and I was too naive to realize I had been a willing pawn in the history of integration.

Chapter 3

All Aboard, Students

**Truth is such a rare thing. It is delightful to tell it.
(Emily Dickerson)**

The first day of school is when the students give you their best attention. Every class should be like the first day. Their feet do not shuffle, and the students have no other desire than to listen to you, their teacher. Students don't even need the bathroom on the first day.

We get lulled into thinking what a wonderful class, but the teacher should continuously check on student engagement in the lesson. I call it the 'train check' or 'who's on board today?' I check to see who is on my train. I am taking a reading of the amount of class engagement in the learning at hand. How many active learners were on board?

It looks like this. In normal conversation with the class about the subject at hand, say, "Stand up, turn around once and sit down." Pause.

Your train riders will follow your instructions. This group of listeners will stand up turn around once and sit down. The daydreaming students will look around the room wondering what happened. Give another command such as do 5 jumping jacks, laugh and sit down. If the students are now participating, you know you have their attention and you may continue the lesson without any acknowledgment of what just happened.

Spend time preparing the lesson, take pride in presenting the lesson to your students and get feedback from them on how well the lesson is being received by the class. Too many times teachers are content to use the lecture method and compliance with the curriculum and justify this by emphasizing the need to get the material covered.

For example: Janice and Judy had classrooms with a connecting small supply closet in between. As Janice talked, a student would set himself a 'challenge' during her lecture. The student would be known to slip out of his desk, creep along the classroom floor, open the door, cross through the supply closet, open Judy's door and try to sneak into her class without being noticed by Janice. Judy would let the student stay rather than interrupt Janice's lesson by returning the escaped student.

As another example: Ma Fike was teaching math to her middle school students in an affluent neighborhood. Before she started each class, she asked all the students who wanted to learn to come down front. She then taught her subclass of students. The school had large windows in those pre-air conditioner days, so the challenge for some students who didn't want to work that day was to sneak out one of the large windows in the back of the class. During one PE class, Judy looked up to see her nephew standing in her class. He said he was there to help with the class.

When she asked him what was up, Donnie said, "Oh, I already knew the material, so I came to help you. Ma Fike won't miss me" and she didn't.

Today, on the news I learned that a teacher had not shown up, nor had a sub been called, so the students were on their own and of course, a fight broke out and it was recorded and posted on the internet. It happened in California, of course.

Gardner's Seven Intelligences but Now Eight

"It's extremely difficult to lead further than you have gone yourself." (Unknown)

Visual: - images, graphics, drawings - a student with this gift becomes one of our artists. Others can take apart a car motor and put it back together, so it even runs, too.

Logical: - deductive and inductive logic facts - a student with this gift can win debates and most arguments. In the workplace, this gift solves problems.

Verbal/linguistic: – words, speaking, writing - a student with this gift will write our suspense novels and become our politicians, good or bad.

Musical/rhythmic: – music, rhythm – where would we be without our songs and all music?

Bodily/Kinesthetic: – art, activity, sports - a student with this gift becomes recognized for amazing art and/or becomes one of our sports heroes, too.

Interpersonal/social: – interact, communicate, talk – a student with this gift becomes a leader, good or bad.

Interpersonal/introspective: – self, solitude, meditate, dream – a student with this gift becomes one of our great thinkers and quiet leaders.

To me interpersonal/social is a gift that needs to be trained to work as an asset rather than how it usually works for some students who go through school with the label 'talks too much'. These are our future speakers, salespersons for high end sales and selling sand to Saudi Arabia. (Yes, the country buys sand.)

There is another intelligence that I believe Gardner should have included. There are eight intelligences not seven. The eighth intelligence is Common Sense.

I remember my mother saying, "Use your common sense." "Think before you act." or "It's your own damn fault for not using common sense."

Common sense to me means 'look at the big picture' to judge if it is sound. What are the consequences if I choose to go ahead with my action? To get better at common sense, use 'stop, look and listen' when your brain comes up with an impulse to do something. Common sense means cause and effect with you in control.

"Keep It Simple, Stupid." (KISS)

The agreement between teachers and students to exhibit a façade of orderly purposefulness is a conspiracy for the least hassle for anyone.
(Unknown)

Back in my own schooldays, finding the mistake in a math problem always put me in a no-win struggle. During the process of adding, subtracting or dividing, but not for multiplication, I would have more mistakes than anyone around me. A favorite for me was erasing the math paper to the point of ripping the paper with my eraser. Then what? Start over? Yes, I had to get a new paper which is frowned upon by the teacher and my peers. I would have to get up, leave my desk and do the walk the shame to get another math paper. Everyone knew I had to use a second piece of math paper.

My eraser was usually worn down to a nub way before the pencil was sharpened to death. Jump ahead to my ninth grade English class for another example. The spelling test was to be done in ink. Any mistake would cost a student a red zero for the week for spelling. I got so many red zeros, I begged my mother to talk to the teacher, which she did. My mother told me that the teacher who made me so frustrated, had said that I wasn't really receiving red zeros in the grade book. What is up with that? The teacher just had a sadistic streak. Teach learning not correcting!

Long Division Practice Tamed

*I've come to the frightening conclusions that I am the decisive element in the classroom. It's my personal approach that creates the climate. It's my daily mood that makes the weather. As a teacher, I possess a tremendous power to make a child miserable or joyous. I can be a tool of torture or an instrument of inspiration. I can humiliate or humor, hurt or heal. In all situations, it is my response that decides whether a crisis will be escalated or deescalated and a child is humanized or dehumanized **(Haim Ginott)***

Long division requires the skill to be checked out by the teacher and immediate feedback given to the student.

Main Dunstable fourth grade teacher, Ms. Peacock, had a great plan for practicing long division. One problem was solved at a time and then checked by the teacher. Instead of just marking it wrong, she pointed out the line where the mistake occurred. Because there was only one problem at a time, the checking went fast without a line being formed where students find other things to amuse themselves.

How do you sell the long division practice time in your math class? It is a game, of course. Become the coach and use encouraging comments such as "almost right" or "oh, so sorry, you have three in a row correct". Point out recurring mistakes such as a times table learned wrongly. Practice multiplying by 0, spacing, maybe graph paper to sort out your lines.

For example: I showed in what line the mistake was, circled the wrong number, showed how to use graph paper for long division, and activated my cheering section. "Only one mistake", "You got two right in a row", "You are on the last row", "Almost done", "This is the same mistake you made last time", "Say 5 times 9 is 45." As the skill progresses, have the teacher's independent students be student checkers. They can check the answer and show the student where the mistake is.

It serves well to cultivate a friendly feeling towards error, to treat it as a companion inseparable from our lives, as something having a purpose, which it truly has. Classroom practice must acknowledge that the stress level for the clueless ones is high. Clues are critical to the clueless.

In reading science or history texts use the same routine. The student answers one question and gets it checked for completeness. Cue your coaching words. For example: "You found three and you need one more." "You found the first one - the hardest one", "You are getting faster at this skill", etc. Send the students back to their seats with hope that they will get the job done quickly. High school reading students love (really) to jump up and check out each other's practice work. Work smart, not hard. (I know – smarter, harder - but it does not sound right.)

Get the Monkey Off Your Back

It has been my experience that wherever you go. there you are.
(Delta Burk)

The teacher asks a student "What is wrong?". At this point, the teacher takes on the problem. It is called a "Monkey on Your Back. Later, another student has a problem, and you repeat the process, letting the student know you will help handle it. By the end of the day, you are covered with 'Monkeys on Your Back' and the sheer weight has you crawling home at the end of the day, exhausted.

To keep the monkeys off her back, the teacher needs to teach students to come up with possible solutions to the problem at hand, the teacher teaches students how to come up with solutions to the student's problem. No monkey is handed over to the teacher and students learn how to problem solve.

Nine Steps to Creativity

We always have time for the things we put first. **(Unknown)**

1. Find new uses

2. Modify – new twist, change meaning, motion, sound, form or order

3. Magnify – (what to add) stronger, longer, thicker, extra value, the plus in the ingredient, duplicate, multiply time (motion) or exaggerate it

4. Minimize - (what you can subtract) volume, smaller, condense, miniature, lower, shorter, lighter, omit it all together, streamline it, split it, understate it

5. Substitute – (who or what else) other ingredient, owner, other approach, other tone of voice

6. Rearrange it – interchange components, layout, other sequence, transpose cause and effect, change place on schedule

7. Reverse – transpose positive and negative values, how about opposites?

8. Adapt – What else is it like? Who can I copy? What else does this suggest?

9. Comfort Zone – Allow yourself to get out of your comfort zone.

Three Minute Cleanse to Unclutter the Mind

Please be patient. I only work here because I am too old for a paper route And too young for social security And too tired to have an affair.
(Unknown)

If the person is not in a place to hear you, your words probably sound like the adults in a Charlie Brown show.

Instead, have the class break into partners in the beginning of class. One partner speaks for three minutes on anything. The listener cannot ask any questions or make comments. The listener can only nod, use empathy, facial expressions and look interested. At the end of three minutes, the listening partner repeats back what was said, remembering as much as possible.

Switch and repeat.

Here are the results: Calm comes quickly and over the class. Each felt listened to and most importunately, ready to focus and learn from the teacher. Three minutes well spent.

Politics at Main Dunstable

I need to be all on fire, for I have mountains of ice to melt.
(William Lloyd Garrison)

The teacher I replaced at Main Dunstable was also my Learning Disabilities Instructor at Riviera College where I received my Master of Education. I assumed she must have left this position to get another that gave her a dedicated room. In hindsight, she may have just gotten away from the evil Jody or maybe been chased out by Jody.

Because of scheduling, I got one of Jody's students, Damon, on my list of students. Damon was a second grader: a verbal, likable student who could not retain anything. The Individual Plan (IEP) said repetition, repetition, repetition. I gave him repetition and more repetition and tried different approaches within the framework of repetition with him.

Jody thought I was not following the IEP strictly enough for her. After all, she wrote it for Damon the year before. Jody went to the principal - not to help Damon - but to regain her self-appointed power.

I was called into the principal's office without any idea of the reason. He said there was no hope for Damon's learning but that he had a soft spot for a pregnant woman, smiled and repeated that he had a soft spot for pregnant women. That was all the help I was getting. That was the first time I learned of her tactics and remained wary of her for the rest of my first year with her.

Earlier in my first year, with a Masters in Learning Disabilities at Main Dunstable, I spoke at a gathering of the Learning Disabilities Parents Evening. I was attempting to explain the options open to parents and how the program worked and that, if they had questions, the parents could call Gail B.

The next day, I was working with my new student in the conference room where it was quiet. Gail B, the director of the Learning Disability program for the county entered to watch my lesson with the students. She observed my instruction with Allan and met with me for a few minutes after Allan left. She wanted to know what I said at the parent meeting.

A parent must have used my explanation to suit her agenda with the director, Gail. Gail accepted my explanation and said I had given a good lesson and I thought she was there because she heard I was a great Learning Disabilities teacher. Politics was rearing its ugly head, again.

As luck would have it, the next year I split my time between two schools, which was fine with me. I only had mornings to be wary of Jody. Broad Street school was run by Nick K. It was an easy fit for me, and I was accepted into the fold of school leaders. Nick K. said he would speak to Peter K, his friend and principal at Main Dunstable School, to lighten up on me.

It was Cam, however, the speech teacher at Broad Street School who sent word to Gail B that I was indeed, a good Learning Disabilities teacher and Cam told her of my ability to synthesize testing and explain the learning problem in concrete terms that made sense to the parents and teachers.

The specialists team: reading, speech, guidance, learning disabled, classroom teacher and principal, met as a team to plan the testing necessary to define the student's strengths and weakness and how it affected the student's learning in the classroom and create a strategy to help.

I was good at putting together the big picture of the student. I would analyze the testing and explain how his/her weakness was hindering the student's progress in the classroom and how to use his/her strengths to overcome his weaknesses.

I had my sights on teaching overseas so I had applied to teach in Bogota, Colombia and I would be leaving at the end of my contract in Nashua. Jody hoped to take one more shot at me. She requested a meeting with Gail B, the Director of Learning Disabilities, my principal and perhaps others.

Gail called me and said, "Don't bother to come to the meeting. You do not need to be there. I will handle it."

After my contract in Bogota, Colombia was up, I had an interview with Galiano, the associate superintendent of Schools in Nashua, where I had taught two years before. He said there were complaints from parents in the past, but of course, he would not elaborate. I met Gail B. to learn what was going on. She said when Galiano was down on a teacher, he would try to make it worse for them, so she called another district and found an opening in North Londonderry and said I should apply. I did, got hired and taught Learning disabilities at my first Middle School setting.

It was ironic that I replaced my instructor when I took the position as an L D teacher at Main Dunstable, N.H. You bet I called on my past learning disabilities experience to help my new students. I had been there and knew a thing or two about good and bad habits. Struggle was good if you had a goal. My goal was to figure out what was not working, create new habits and practice, practice, practice. "It takes 21 days to learn a new habit and most give up on day 17."

How could I be in the "in crowd" teaching at Broad Street School and be so much in the "out crowd" teaching at Main? At the end of my year at Londonderry Junior High, I went to teach in Oberursal, Germany.

Chapter 4

A Simple Blueprint to Fix the Spiral Curriculum Model Problem

Knowledge becomes wisdom only after it has been put to practical use. (Unknown)

While teaching at Frankfurt International School (FIS) in Germany, I was given a few days off to meet with other teachers to develop a curriculum that would define what skills, in which grade the skills would be introduced, in what grades the skill would be practiced and in what grade mastery of the skill would be expected. The concept was new to me but elegant in its simplicity.

Instead of teachers teaching the skill, practicing the skill, and moving on when some students had not mastered the skill, each grade level teacher now knew which skills needed to be mastered by the end of the year. The responsibility for the skill becomes defined and shared with all the elementary teachers.

It is a paradigm shift from the spiral curriculum where everyone teaches the same skill, just believing the skill has been taken to a higher level during the next grade level. Teachers now had a more unified handle on the elementary school curriculum.

I had the pleasure of running the Elementary Learning Center at FIS, known as ELC (pronounced ELK). I was a resource room teacher for students who were having academic problems in one of the classes, from kindergarten through six grades. Some students were German,

Japanese and many other nationalities, but most were American students of American businessmen or diplomats who wanted a U.S. curriculum for their children while their parents were serving and moving on to new assignments in other countries.

How to Sound out Long Words If Phonics Lets You Down

People change. The times change, too. The value of an Educated Mind, worthwhile work and community service endure. ***(Unknown)***

It was in the ELC Center at FIS that someone came up with how to sound out long words if you don't have a good grasp of phonics. The name of the book was 'Phonics in Proper Perspective' by Arthur W. Heilman. Copyright 1964. I had been carrying this from one teaching assignment to the next since college.

I decided to give mastering phonics another try. I had given up on trying to learn the dictionary pronunciation key many times in the past and just the mention of diphthongs freezes me like a deer in headlights.

I found my rusted paper clip on page 78. The chapter was syllabication, and there were rules to divide a word up into syllables. It was my breakthrough to teaching phonics to sight readers. There were less rules and exceptions to the rules. Divide a word between double consonants. (cvvc). I was forty years old and just learning that there was a rule for this.

Prefixes came next - so many of them. I had until then only mastered 'dis' and 'un' even though I had taken Latin in high school for two years. Suffixes were an eye opener, too. I at least knew 'ment' as in 'government'. Strange as it seems it was during this time that I realized that 'meant' sounded like '-ment' - but it had an 'a' in it. I wondered how long I had been spelling meant with the 'a' left out.

Here is the overview of the big picture. Long vowels seemed to be easier to learn, so I would have the student start with the long sound and then the short sound. By saying the vowels in pairs, long vowel sound first and then short sounds, students seemed to be able to get closer to the short sound by saying the long sound first and then the short sound for the same vowel.

Next, students learned the common prefixes and practiced identifying the common ones for grade level, pronouncing them and learning the meaning.

Then students learned the suffixes common for their grade level and their meaning; and practiced recognizing the prefixes in words, too. You have now isolated the root word.

Now, look for patterns within the letters. Learn and practice dividing words between double consonants. Vowel, consonant, consonant vowel (vccv) is the pattern. Now for the vowel. If the vowel is in the middle of the first syllable it will usually be short. If the vowel is at the end of the first syllable it will usually be long. The students practice saying the word with a long vowel sound and then a short vowel sound. Many students will, at this point, recognize the word from their oral language vocabulary; meaning that the word is in their long-term memory, and they know for sure if the vowel is long or short. (Students have a speaking vocabulary, listening vocabulary and reading vocabulary.) For the students who do not recognize the word, the student decides which sounds better or is easier to say.

At this point, many students realize that the tongue has a great deal of influence over whether the word follows the rule or becomes one of the many insane exceptions to the rules.

The next pattern is consonant, vowel, consonant (cvc). Students practice using the long vowel sound and short vowel sound. The check is which sounds better to the ear. Which was easier to say?

My ninth-grade students at THS would have competitions pronouncing words correctly that they had never heard of before.

Maslow would agree that "the student has become less teacher-dependent", Montessori would say "the student did it without help from the teacher", and Confucius would say the "student can explain it to others".

Finding the Magic Bullet

It is the greatest inequity to try to make unequal things equal
(Unknown)

My son's fourth grade teacher would send students back to their seat to correct a long division problem; but finding the mistake in the problem always put a student in a no-win struggle.

My own experience as a child doing long division was that in a short amount of time, I would have more mistakes than when I started. A favorite for me was erasing the math paper to the point of ripping the paper with my eraser. Then what? Start over? Yes! was my answer and I had to do the walk of shame to get a new sheet of math paper. The class will know I failed my first attempt and wasting paper was never overlooked by your peers.

Acknowledging the stress level for the clueless was the first step. Clues were critical to the clueless. In math practice, I showed in what line the mistake was, circled the wrong number, showed how to use graph paper for long division and activated my cheering section: "Only one mistake", "You got two right in a row", "You are on the last row", "Almost done", "This is the same mistake you made last time", "Say 5 times 9 is 45". As the skill progresses, I have the teacher's independent students be helpers. They would check the answer and show the student where the mistake was.

This style of practice worked well in reading skills as well. For example, ask students to find all the reasons found in a literature, history or science class chapter or even a paragraph. Cue the cheering section from the coach. "Well, done", "You found three and you need one more", "You found the first one, the hardest one", "You are getting faster at this skill", etc.

High school reading students loved to jump up and check out other students' practice. I call it social dynamics - used not abused. "It is well to cultivate a friendly feeling towards error; to treat it as a companion inseparable from our lives, as something having a purpose, which it truly has. Work smarter not harder".

Student Yelling as He Reads

*Education demands, then, only this: the utilization of the inner powers of the child for his own instruction. (**Montessori**)*

Our second-grade teacher, Mary Lamb, said she had a student who read out loud in his strong, outdoor voice. It was driving the teacher crazy. My number one goal was to get the teacher to reveal her pet peeve about the student. It was not hard for Mary to come up with it. Step two was to find the time in the schedule to have the cute redheaded German boy, Waldo (who reminded me of a young Boris Becker from tennis fame) come to me in the learning center. Step two was quite important - to let the teacher decide when one of their students was to miss class as there was never a good time, but you wanted the teacher to make that decision.

For step three you needed to have the student leave the class, walk to the learning center across the school campus and arrive on time at the learning center. I put a small analog clock on Waldo's desk with the time set to his departure time. He and the other younger students would match the wall clock with the time for leaving and leave without disrupting the class or having the teacher remind the student.

I asked Waldo if he knew why he was here, and he said "no". I explained to him that he was reading out loud in his outside strong voice and it was driving his teacher crazy. He didn't know what I meant; so, I had him read out loud for me and we practiced reading quietly at different volumes. We picked the volume that would be acceptable for him. He told me he read out loud to remember what he read so it was important to pick the softest voice that helped him do that. He had to listen to himself read in order to make sense of the text and remember it.

When he was ready to try reading quietly in class, step 4 came into play. He was to tell his teacher he was practicing reading with a softer voice. Before he came to ELC each day, he had to ask his teacher if he had read softly enough. All the teachers had to say was "yes" or "no". I had told the teacher that he would be coming to her and telling her he was practicing reading softer, and he would ask for a "yes" or "no" each day before he left for ELC.

I knew it was working when Waldo showed up breathless, with a "yes" from his teacher and a great big smile. I would return to the teacher to ask if he was practicing reading softer and leaving without disrupting the class. I then asked for the next thing that was bothering the teacher. In this case she said that was all. She smiled and said what a sweet boy he was. I knew then that the two of them were on the same page and all was going to be well in the teacher/student relationship. They could work out their problems together. Waldo became a real student in her class. They had a bond, a positive relationship; and the Learning Center and I were out of one more student. Of course, this sounds so Mary Poppins now that you have read through it. What is the catch, you ask?

I ran a store in the Elementary Learning Center (known as ELC) that opened one day a week for the first ten minutes of the class. Not only did it work but worked with no money spent by me. I put out the word for used items that kids might want for themselves or as a gift for someone. I got splendid travel posters from the travel agency, items teachers or parents had at home and any place I heard of who could offer free contributions.

One item was a knickknack, given to me by Mrs. Fenner, a first-grade teacher. A student bought the knickknack with her tickets and gave it to Mrs. Fenner as a gift of love. Yes, it was true. The teacher got back her own knickknack that she had contributed to the ELC store.

The store was a powerful tool because the students received many tickets during their daily time in the ELC. One ticket for coming on time, one for getting a "yes" from his or her teacher and many tickets for each time I saw them practicing a habit that we agreed to work on.

The new habit was tailored just for the individual student and had been agreed upon by the student and me while in the ELC.

Again, the pattern was repeated in classrooms throughout K – 6 at the International School, FIS. Here is a summary of steps.1. Referral from the teacher - verbal or written - about a student. 2. Learn the pressing problem from the teacher. Was there a pet peeve? There were usually 3. Agree on the problem the student would practice, in discussion with the student, of course. 4. Practice the new habit in ELC, 5. Transfer the new habit to the classroom. 6. Feedback collected over time from the student, teacher and me. 7. My goal was to learn that "He was doing fine" through the teacher's smile. Once the first pet peeve has been resolved, a bond between the student and teacher is established and the remaining pet peeves go away.

Each student worked independently on an individual ELC assignment, sometimes math facts, reading skills, handwriting and any habit we learned was a hindrance to having a good day in class.

Handwriting Magic for a Kinder Student

*The real menace in dealing with a five-year-old, is that in no time at all, you begin to sound like a five-year-old. **(Unknown)***

While teaching at the Elementary Learning Center (ELC) there was a tiny Kinder student who was referred because of a fine motor problem that showed up in her handwriting. I asked Wendy if she knew why she was seeing me. She said "no", and I explained that her teacher was worried about her handwriting. I gave her the primary handwriting paper and asked her to write her name.

Wow! It was a mess with different size letters, inconsistent spacing and not grounded on a line. By grounding, I mean starting the down stroke for the capital letter under the first blue and ending by touching the second blue line. The middle of the dotted line was where the small letter began. I folded the paper on the first blue line. Then I folded the paper on the second blue line. I made a third fold on the dotted line. She folded the paper like I did with some help from me. I said use the lines for your letters.

Well, we wrote her name using the three lines as her guide. We next compared both of her efforts by placing the papers side by side. I asked her which one she liked best. Of course, she picked her second effort. You could see a 'lightbulb moment' unfolding in Wendy's mind. She hadn't noticed the three lines until now. We practiced for a few days in the ELC center. She was drawing the letters slowly. When she showed mastery of using the lines as her guide after only a couple of practice sessions, I asked her to try using the lines in her class. By now she was relaxed and enjoying the blue line 'trick' and, you guessed it, her handwriting improved greatly in the classroom on her own after a couple of lessons in the ELC. I did not see her again.

Later, after I was fired by the principal but not the director of FIS, Dr. Gibbons, I learned from her mother that she had written a letter to the director stating that I had cured her daughter's school problems in a few lessons in the ELC center. Was she ready to go for the next 12 years on her own?

Writing Needs a Concrete Map to Creativity

If we are forced at every hour to watch or listen to horrible events, this constant stream of impressions will deprive, even the most delicate among us, all respect for humanity. ***(Cicero at the height of the Roman Empire)***.

When learning how to write for the state writing test, I heard someone say, "Tell them what you are going to tell, tell them, and tell them what you told them."

So that's what writing is about. That's the big picture in a nutshell. While teaching in Bogota, I learned writing was like a train. Connect each new sentence to a word from the sentence you just written. That's how you get from one sentence to the next.

There is an actual list of transitions to use when you change to the next subject. Once you have written a sentence or a couple of sentences, it's time to change the subject, hence a new transition. That is how a paragraph is formed. It was now clear; I needed a story map to make writing concrete. Demystify writing with a road map. From this map, the student can go on to a proper paragraph essay.

For example: Granddaughter number two did not spell easily and did not write well. I had the good fortune to explain how to write to Lily, my precious granddaughter. It went like this:

"Why are you mad at me, Lily?"

Lily said, "Because you are making me write."

Gramma said, "That is your topic. That is your title, too."

Gramma said, "Why do you not want to write? That is your first sentence."

Lily said, "I hate to write because I don't like to write."

Gramma said," And two reasons you do not like to write are?" Those are your three sentences for your paragraph with each sentence connected to the previous sentences by using a word from the previous sentence. Tell me again why you do not want to write. That is your conclusion and last sentence. You told me what you were writing. You gave me three reasons why you don't like to write. You told me what you were going to say. You said it in three sentences. You told me what you said. You said it in one sentence. Congratulations, you now know what is in a paragraph. You now know how to write. Was it painful?"

Lily said, "Yes."

The Story Map has everything on one sheet of paper. It is like a writing app on paper. On this map there is room for the topic, title (gotten from the topic), three sentences, conclusion sentence, a transition for each new group of sentences from the transition sheet, point of view (first person, second person or third person) and of course, the tense (present, past or future).

The Story Map was a great visual outline that gives the creative process structure.

Wilma Got Him Hooked

Genius is the power of lighting one's own fire. **(Unknown)**

A parent came to me saying her son did not read well and did not like to read. The referral for evaluation was more from the parent than his teacher. He was another sight reader who struggled to read enough to please his mother. Each day, he came into the Elementary Learning center (ELC) and read to my assistant, Wilma, from his own book. When he came to a word, Wilma gave him the pronunciation of the word. He was a sight reader and he was not asked to sound out the word.

At the end of year meeting with his mother, she said he now likes to read. She went on to say that I had assured her in our first meeting that I would get him to like reading. It sounded like I made a promise that I might have easily broken. It also sounded like Wilma put in the effort to move a reading hater into a reading liker.

Politics at FIS

*The child is much more spiritually elevated than is usually supposed. He often suffers, not from too much work, but from work that is unworthy of him. (**Montessori**)*

Herb S., the principal, put me on his hit list for some reason we never learned. I had happy parents and classroom teachers and I helped develop the FIS curriculum changes making concrete suggestions for how the grade skills could be introduced, which grades were for practice of the skill and in what grade the skill should be expected to be mastered. I played tennis at the same courts and same time as he did. I played tennis every week with his wife next to Herb's court and I loved my job.

My headmaster, Dr Gibbons, did not accept Herb's request of not renewing my contract and had Herb and me meet again. This time, Herb said I was unprofessional; actually, the most unprofessional teacher he had ever met. I will let you evaluate for yourself.

I was coaching my son's baseball team. Unfortunately, open house and his first game were on the same night. Because parents traditionally visit the classroom teachers first and if enough time was left, they would seek out the specialists, I offered to start my son's first ball game in Germany. I would leave the game early and arrive at school in time to be in my room after classroom teacher time was over. He agreed, but when we had to meet again on the order of Dr. Gibbons, he spent the time saying I was the most unprofessional teacher he had met. He also said he didn't like me helping to match up Learning Disabilities students with an appropriate teacher the next year.

A short time later, Herb was no longer principal at that school and still later, couldn't cope with his debilitating disease, so he shot himself.

Chapter 5

Clay's Bad Habit

Being ignorant is not so shameful as being unwilling to learn. (unknown)

My aunt Helen asked me to help her son, Clay, my cousin. I went to his school and met with his teacher to learn of her concerns about Clay's delayed academic progress. The teacher was concerned about his handwriting. She could not read it.

Ah, an easy fix I thought. I can fix his handwriting problem, so I asked Clay on our first session, "Did you know your handwriting cannot be read by your teacher?" This is what Clay told me? He said he had to copy stuff from the board. He didn't have time to look at the board and write everything down, so he just wrote down what he saw without looking at his paper. His goal was to hand in the assignment to the class and he did that.

Of course, I told the teacher of his system for copying. The teacher must have made a comment to Clay and Clay told his mother. His mother told me that he didn't need any help and that was the end. From an LD teacher's perspective, he had a problem spelling the word so he could not capture the whole word with his eyes, send the word to short term memory, look at the paper, find the correct place and retrieve the word that he needed to copy from the board from his short-term memory.

Clay fixed his problem by copying from the board and writing the whole assignment without looking at the paper and of course, he got tagged with unreadable handwriting.

He also needed to learn tricks to keep his place on the paper while he was looking at the board. His spelling problem was compounded by not having a good system for tracking his place on the paper.

What is a teacher to do but feel frustrated? (No one should write so badly at his age). Why didn't the elementary teachers teach him to write when they had him? She thinks of her 30 other students. Maybe she was not trained to teach handwriting and held it against the student. What is a parent to do when her son was probably called out by the teacher, but to end the tutoring?

On a side note, I was to tutor one of his peers - my other cousin, Lenny. Before I got to start tutoring Lenny, his mother, Aunt Edie, told me she had changed her mind about tutoring. She must have spoken to Helen. For the rest of their school years both stayed in the "dumb classes."

Chapter 6

There are Only Four Personalities

Wit is educated insolence. (Aristotle)

Four personalities: supporter = S, Introvert detailed person = C, Notice me = I, Full steam ahead. Straight = D

In a workshop called Teacher Effective Training in Orlando, Fl, taught by Rick Roach, I learned about a simple personality test. You start with the premise that there are only four personality groups.

The S group are the supporters of the world. S personalities reach out, comfort and want everyone to be nice. Families are their grounding. Within moments of meeting an S personality she will have out her wallet showing you the family and pets. In the workplace, this personality brings in home cooked sweet rolls and is a team player who does not make waves.

The opposite is the D group, the leaders of the world. He/she is going full steam ahead, driven to succeed, someone who must achieve, a leader. If you met one, he/she would be in a power blue suit and driving a black Mercedes. In the workplace, this personality wants to be in charge and assumes he/she is.

The C group are represented by Felix Unger in the Odd Couple. They are detail oriented; many are number crunchers. The C personality is not a good team player because he/she would rather work alone. Pretty much a nerd in the workforce.

The I group are the entertainers of the world. "Notice me!" comes to mind. They like a good time even while they work. At the workplace, he/she is fun to have around, but if only he/she would stop cracking jokes.

A new school, called Dr. Phillips High. Dr Phillips was an affluent community. Bill was hired to be the principal. He was an 'I' personality. He had an outgoing personality and people liked to be around him. Unfortunately, he hired those most like him. The brand-new school opened without hiring any teacher leaders. There was no one to send out the get well soon cards and organize the goodies for faculty gatherings. There were no bean counters counting the cash and no one who could draw up a master schedule for the place.

I was amazed to hear this about a real place. My son went there. When my son got home from school one day, I asked "What happens if you come in late to school?"

He said, "Oh, no big deal, just bring the teacher a doughnut and all is well." Who was taking attendance? I wondered. He liked his school. Everyone was laid back.

When picking grade levels or simple committees, shop for one of each group. The D assumes leadership and assigns the C person to get it done. The S is the mediator to keep the flow going nicely. Everyone will be happy. Then I will offer comic relief and know the best happy hour.

Dream Job at Laurel Oaks Hospital

Nothing in the world can take the place of persistence.
(Calvin Coolidge)

I had the wonderful opportunity of being hired by Laurel Oaks Hospital. I was an Orange County teacher working at a private hospital. The director hired me to teach English to students who were under hospital care. The students were under psychological care and stayed until their insurance ran out - whether cured or not. We had three wings; One wing was for the depressed students; one was for 'acting out' students and the third wing was for drug addiction.

It seemed logical to develop individual programs because each of my classes had students from grade six through twelve. In this model, students are responsible for choosing their level of vocabulary and literature book. We switched from grade level material to skill level material without stigma. I used the Goldilocks rule. "If you pick a book that is too easy, you will like the easy work, but the excitement will wear off and you will be wasting your time. If you pick a book that is too hard, you will quit working because you will have bored yourself to death. Pick a book that is neither too easy nor too hard. Pick one that is just right for you. Your goal is to take back good grades to add to the grades you already have at your regular school."

"If there are five words on the page in the literature section that you do not know, the book is too hard for you." I spoke.

The vocabulary lesson consisted of four pages with the first page dedicated to words, meanings and a quiz. I had students use the teacher's edition answer book to correct his/her own quiz at his/her seat. It seemed sensible to complete the remaining exercises after checking and correcting your quiz. Why learn it wrongly, when you can practice using the correct word? Use the correct word while you finish the rest of the unit. Learn it right. "Teach teaching not correcting." (Montessori) Worked like a charm.

With a ridiculously small class count, it was a "no brainer" to accept the concept of honesty as the norm. The degree of difficulty was student choice. The questions on the literature were constructed by me. I corrected the rest of the pages in the vocabulary book myself, put a grade on it for the student and entered it in the grade book.

The students were not judged by their grade level but by a self-evaluation of their own skill level, and that judgment call was student-led, not a top-down teacher decision. My class was pretty much stress-free and so was I. I had a view of the courtyard outside my desk side window - the only window. My nylons didn't run when brushed up against the shiny new desks and all my desk top teacher stuff matched. We teachers were served a sirloin steak weekly.

I gave equal weight to the student's commitment to the education processes and the student's agenda. The student had to deal with himself, peers and the home unit, psychiatrist, parents, siblings, etc. There was no homework. I expected consistent effort and realistic work production and making improvements in my class. The grades were good because the students were not learning on frustration level, nor were the students working on their mastery level. They were learning on their practice level, so cheating became a non-issue. A stress-free job turned into a no win for me.

In hindsight, I realized I did not follow the lead of the principal and other teachers. At our weekly meeting the teachers would complain about the students and the principal supported that way of thinking. Drama, drama, drama was in. When asked how the troublesome student was doing in my class, my answer was that the student was doing fine - no problems. I knew my answer was not in sync with others' expectations and it should have been good news that the student was having success somewhere; but neither teachers nor principal wanted to know what I was doing to get the results that I did. The weekly meetings were a waste of my time. I had to listen to my peers complaining about the kids without offering solutions. One teacher in particular was into power, so the students got into being oppositional defiant to him. Not a good mix and a disaster waiting to happen daily in his room.

I knew politics had arrived at my job when the evaluator/supervisor from Orange County Schools asked me to teach a whole class lesson. Remember the students were from six grade to twelfth grade and dealing with their issues. What I did wrong was not telling the students we had to put on a 'dog and pony' show for my supervisor.

Instead, I sprung it on them, and they were resentful not to be doing their regular work routines and confused by the sudden change. One student refused to participate, and I had to call for a worker from their unit to come get the student.

I did not have three years at the same school, no continuing contract or any other recourse. My supervisor's boss said I could apply for other positions in the county, which I did. One principal called me back and said I had a problem at the county Human Resource Dept., and he could not offer me the position he had planned on offering me. So much for being told I could apply to other positions.

I had students write their final words to me on their last day at the hospital. I found out I told funny stories and was appreciated. I don't remember telling stories, but I remember giving witty tidbits of life such as, "It takes 21 days to learn a new habit and most give up on day seventeen." (Anonymous) I remember explaining to my anarchy student that he was a conformist because he wore the standard black raincoat, black boots, wore his hair long and stringy and displayed the anarchy symbol in red, which was 'in' at the time. He was shocked and laughed at how he had missed that. He was a conformist. He was off to find a new cause. I do remember saying "Never teach a pig to sing. It's a waste of time and besides it annoys the pig."

My last two months were going to be a hassle for me, so I went out on disability and rested my ruptured disc. Good-bye dream job, but I escaped the politics. I did think to have my students' final goodbye to me copied and put in my file at the county office.

Chapter 7

The Tragic Tragedy of the Paradigm Shift in Education to Middle School

There is evil in Education. I found it and survived.
(F. Atwood)

"The greatest crime that society commits is that of wasting the money which it should use for children on things that will destroy them and society itself, as well." (Montessori)

We educators allowed the 'Middle School concept' to be unleashed upon all the world. Teachers are still wondering how it happened. The Middle School, or 'Junior High' concept understood that students needed structure, sports (either as a player and/or spectator) and social clubs to give a sense of belonging and learning how to give to others in the community, as well.

Instead, this breathtakingly ignorant assumption that this was the way to go simply rules out any logic and common sense. A window metaphor comes to mind. Keep the window half open between the teacher and the student for communicating and between teacher and the administrator. Well, the whole window and window frame was given to the parents and the students. The pecking order was redefined. It would now be parents at the top, students second and teachers last. Don't hurt a student's feelings but make them feel good about themselves, regardless.

No longer did Middle School have to supply the expensive support umbrella for the sports programs of the former Junior High era. Gone now were the days when you got into trouble as a student in school; you would be in just as much trouble, or more, when you went home. Gone were the expensive social and community clubs' frameworks (most necessary for this age group) and its liability costs, as well.

Enter the world of madness. Students now went to their moms with a complaint as soon as they got home. Actually, the students can call the parent right from class nowadays. The mom would then call the principal on speed dial, right away. The principal will then call you in the next day and you, the teacher, would be reprimanded. The principal now supports all parent complaints at the expense of what is right and wrong.

The complaints stop at the principal level and no longer get to bother anyone at the county level because it was part of the new Middle School ideology and supported by the superintendent, who found a way to end the complaints going to the county level and bothering the superintendent.

The teacher now teaches with students using their phones in class, head down on the desk, teaching with classroom chatter going on in the background and worst of all, knowing your "teacher words" could be twisted - words taken out of context and reported to mom who then calls the principal who calls in the teacher and issues a reprimand.

To keep the principal at bay many teachers worked to keep a student complaint from making it to the principal's office. Students could only receive 50% instead of a zero for no credit. Homework was assigned but the students were no longer held accountable. Extra credit was freely given to a student whose grades were in danger. Too many student failures were now the teacher's problem. One solution was that teachers pretended to teach, and students pretended to learn.

The teachers were now able to be micromanaged by the principal. Teachers were now able to be told how to teach, told what is allowed in class and what is not; told what must be written on your black board or white board daily; what you can say to a student and what a student could now say to you, the teacher, and get away with. New teachers were put through a year of busy work which became added to the file on them. Sarcasm was out but it happens to be a sophisticated control and to make harmless wit takes talent. Sarcasm is mainly distinguished by the inflection with which it is spoken.

Schools now need: individual cell phones for administrators, computers to take home, gas credit cards and daily police presence in the school to deal with fighting students and drugs. How about: workshops for administrators that include a plane ticket, lodging and meals; buying china and decorations to put on luncheons for other principals; buying new books on a rotating schedule because it is time for new books rather than if the new books are needed; the county School Board paying for certain teachers to take college courses, masters or even doctorate classes; making a single office somewhere in the county responsible for the temperature setting in your individual room; purchasing software based on the perks given to you by the company instead of the versatility of the software; moving out established department leaders to other schools, always announced on Friday afternoon; putting teacher assistants in situations where they can report on the teacher; getting rid of teachers who question nefarious acts; daily sign-in sheets for teachers in the main office; no day off before a holiday; making class pets a liability; being in the hall to monitor the students who are changing class in the hall at the same time as monitoring the students already in your class. One of the other Learning Disabilities teachers got free periods off during the day because the teacher did not want the free team teacher in the classroom. Stealing from each other or from teachers became an area that was no longer investigated. The resources were now used to break up fights and arrest students for breaking the law at school. Who had time to investigate stealing?

What do You Mean? I Always Act Like This.

What do you mean? I always act like this. They always pass me.
(Andrea)

A small Hispanic seventh grader coded 'Learning Disabled' came to class each day with a routine to drive any teacher crazy. He was a good-looking young adolescent with a charming smile and so entertaining to his friends. The class would bound into the math class, go to the back, listen and wait for Andrea's show.

Now that I am teaching students and not just the material, I did home visits with my students. Busted. In Andrea's sparse bedroom, there was a wall displaying all his Karate belts. He could focus, he could concentrate, he could learn. Basically, he had played us.

I called him on his "school act" and he replied, "What do you mean? I always act like this. They always pass me."

I thought it was true that he was passed along every year just to see him go. I requested he now bring to class the karate boy personality who knew how to listen, pay attention and learn. Gone was the Ritalin, too.

I had asked him how he acted in other classes. Of course, he said "fine" and of course I asked his elective teacher Sandy S. and told her about Andrea's success in his out of school karate life; which led to me taking him to Sandy's room during the class change over. I introduced her to his other personality and explained she could expect Andrea to bring his Karate personality each day, which allowed him to become a positive addition to her class. He was my introduction to Middle School and co-teaching.

At this time, in the downward spiral of the field of Learning Disabilities, the bureaucrats who had taken over the direction of the Learning Disabilities sphere had moved on from the one-on-one model, past the Resource Model and on to the Inclusive Model.

In this model, the learning-disabled teacher had to move from class to class with the students. It was more like keeping the low-performing students together in the same class and send an L.D. teacher with them. It was called 'team teaching', but it was in name only.

In one of our classes, we were grouped at the back of the class. It made it easier to help students when they were together, but the back of the class never mingled with the front of the room students and neither did the teacher interact with the back of the room students. Actually, she taught with the overhead projector and did not interact with any students, front or back. She liked me because I ran the back of the class, and nothing interfered with her lesson plan at the overhead projector.

I Statement

I know that you believe you understand what you think I said, but I am not sure you realize that what you heard is not what I meant.
(Unknown)

When you_________it makes me feel_________because _________.

For example: When you sit in class and refuse to work, it makes me feel useless as your teacher because I don't know what it would take to get you to stop sleeping in class.

There are three things to do to make this work. First, you must sit in front of your student in straight chairs with both sets of knees close but not touching. Secondly, ask only one question. For example: First, say the 'I' statement. Ask this question "What would it take to get you to not sleep in class?" Thirdly, you may not say anything else. Finally, remain silent. The waiting will kill you 'so to speak, but don't speak.'

When the silence becomes too much for you, repeat the 'I' statement and question. When the student says, "I don't know" repeat the 'I' statement or just the question. When a student says something, be quiet but put an interested look on your face.

In a short amount of time, the student will start giving excuses or reasons but, in general, they will tell you what the problem is and what the solution can be. The student will come up with a solution or two for solving the problem. After all, it is the student's problem. Together, agree to try out the best solution and meet again the next day.

The Choking Pencil Grip

Never let anything mechanical know when you are in a hurry.
(Unknown)

Back in my second-grade class as a student, we were called up to Mrs. Battle's desk to sign our report card before taking it home to show our parents. I had never gone to the teacher's desk. It was only for those who needed help. I didn't. I was told I was smart. Each of us had to write our name, in our best cursive handwriting, on a line on our report card.

For the first time, I saw my handwriting. Using my fat primary green pencil with no eraser, I wrote out Freida. I was horrified to see fat heavy huge letters of different sizes. I used up all the space allotted and more. I had never noticed my handwriting before and there I was expecting some praise from Ms. Battles; but she said nothing. I remember thinking as I walked back to my desk, "I failed writing." I couldn't write.

I had not been conscious that I could not write neatly but I was conscious that my coloring was impeccable. What was up with that? I always stayed in the lines and kept an even pressure with each stroke.

Six years of Penmanship lessons in the future did not ever make me feel good about my penmanship. I never got a 'good penmanship' certificate in any grade. In hindsight, I practiced during penmanship lessons and wrote my usual way in my everyday seat work. I never wondered why it didn't transfer but I was "smart" and had to get the work done fast.

If only someone had pointed out that my pencil grip was excessive. In my small second grade mind, I had come up with the idea of holding my pencil tightly and with intense concentration, hoping to control my letters, size and spacing. All I got was a cramped hand and a giant callus on my middle finger on my left hand.

One day in my sixth grade, my teacher called out Fred's name to get his paper. No Fred in class. It was Freida. Oh, the public humiliation. "Persistent in error is a sign of a fool." (Anonymous)

The fat green pencils are mostly gone from the modern curriculum, so numerous students now use a three-finger grip; whereas I was assigned only a choice of one grip. We were of the standardized age. There was only one way, and the teacher knew best.

In my case and most other cases, the poor handwriting is passed on in a gene down the family tree. My grandfather had poor handwriting while my grandmother had tiny, tiny impeccable script. My father, his brother and two of my brothers had poor handwriting, along with my son and one of his daughters. My son's other two daughters had tiny, tiny impeccable writing. I lost out in that gene pool. Actually, our 'poor handwriting' family members had the same, easily recognizable style. The genes were in control.

Through my elementary years, I would be mesmerized by watching the teacher write on the board. (Overhead projectors had not been invented.) Later when I began teaching, I could not write on the board with my left hand but I could write on the board with my right hand.

It all came together after I got my masters in Learning Disabilities. When I saw a student using the bad habit I'd developed in second grade, I would pull the pencil out of his hand and yell "You are choking your pencil to death. Loosen the grip.".

I would show the student the ever present callous on my left hand and ask if his hand got sore; knowing the answer beforehand. We then practiced not too tight and not too loose, but just right; trying out different slants of the paper, types of pencils, grips and fat pens. The student and I would put together a plan to design a better handwriting system by changing the variables and getting rid of bad habits.

Handwriting which is part of a small motor control is a big deal and can have a lasting effect on some students' psyche. On the other hand, I excel at pencil sketching, painting, carving and lathe work. Teach students to learn their strengths and weaknesses.

Chapter 8

The Great Awaking

**Sexual harassment in this area will not be reported.
However, it will be graded. (Unknown)**

The plan was to get a master's in Education Leadership but for no known reason it became a Learning Disabilities course. Nonetheless, the awaking happened. Medical students would read of symptoms and more often than not, conclude that they indeed had that disease. The more I read, the more symptoms I had. I finally got it.

In my case it came through loud and clear. I went through school with Learning Disabilities. The term hadn't been invented until after my school years as a student. All the red flags were there: no phonics, bad speller, poor handwriting, poor grip, could not take notes in class because I would forget what the teacher was saying. I was too busy fumbling around in my brain trying to spell. Impossible subtraction flash cards, losing my attention while reading, stressful, sweaty palms, knot in stomach, difficulty learning another language, forgetting the beginning of the sentence by the time I got to the end of the sentence.

I still remember sitting in second grade with the small white composition paper in front of me. The directions were to write about anything, and I had nothing in my brain. Not even the first sentence. What was wrong with me? I was supposed to be smart. Well, my instructor at Riviera said I should take a writing course to learn how to write. She could have pointed out to me that I was L.D. and use me as an example in our weekly classes.

Politics at GMS

*Education should therefore include the two forms of work, manual and intellectual, for the same person, and thus, make it understood by practical experience that these two kinds complete each other and are equally essential to a civilized existence. **(Unknown)***

I was hired by Bill W. but he left during the summer and Beth, the new principal, called me in to have a chat. We had a chat and I felt I was off to a good year, but Beth was brought in to change the junior high concept to the Middle School concept. She chose 'down and dirty' to dismantle an older entrenched faculty who treated each other as family.

Beth had Terry C. come out from the county office and observe me. Terry C. was head of Learning Disabilities. She never spoke to me, but Beth told me that Terry C. said I talked in monotone speech.

My first year was over and I was re-hired because no observation of my teaching was made by Beth in the allotted time set by contract. I won on a technicality.

I was offered any school in the county by the union if I went away quietly, but I said I wanted to return to Glenridge. I did. Beth gave me a big smile at the first faculty meeting of the year as I said I was glad to be back at Glenridge. I was wondering what she would come up with this year to rid the school of me.

I had not thought of this one and did not see it coming. Beth had Joe, one of her assistant principals, call in my home room students individually to say a swear word one at a time and ask if I had said that word. The best she came up with was that I said "hell" and "damn" which was not ever true.

She called in my assistant from my one Learning Strategies class who told her I said I had to put on a 'dog and pony' show for Beth's observation. It was true. I did say it. My assistant was pulled often for other assignments without my knowing. I stopped making plans for my assistant because she only showed up randomly. Beth got in her required observation on time. I did not have a continuing contract, so no reason needed to be given to let me go. Silly me. I thought good wins over evil.

Beth had someone in the county personnel office put a '16' next to my name to be seen only by prospective principals. The 16 was part of the secret code used by the administrators to warn other principals about a problem teacher. It meant "Don't hire". She found out where I was interviewing, called and said I had a lawsuit with my former employer. She must have spoken to Whyne E., my current principal in a new county, while they were on an expense-paid trip to a book company in Arizona.

On his return, he did a one eighty on me and stopped talking to me. She had used overkill and had me blacklisted in three counties; which was hard on the interview process because I was unaware of this.

As luck would have it, Joe got fired from the county for messing with the college reimbursement vouchers. His wife went with him. The county was funding his next degree. Terry Click got brain cancer and Beth died after eating a Costco hot dog. She thought she was having indigestion, but she really had a heart attack and died while spending the night in the reclining living room chair.

Memories and Your Eyes

*When you fall in a river, you're no longer a fisherman: You are a swimmer. (**Gene Hill**)*

The story goes like this. Clyde likes his job, and the company likes him. Soon Clyde is promoted to vice president of sales. Part of his new job description is to hire greatly needed salesmen and he needed them fast. Sales were going through the roof.

Clyde had been interviewed before, but he had not done any interviewing of others. During Clyde's first interview, he was distracted by Fred's eyes. Clyde got distracted by Fred's eye movement. When Clyde asked Fred a question, Fred's eyes kept shooting to the side, mostly to the left corner of his left eye, but sometimes to the right. Suddenly, it hit Clyde what was wrong. Fred had shifty eyes. He knew shifty eyes meant dishonesty and now he knew he was not hiring anyone with shifty eyes. When he came across a salesperson with shifty eyes, he fired them.

Clyde went about his business and hired several new people, but sales stopped dramatically. Clyde had bad brain information. He hired visual learners because those people did not have shifty eyes.

Unfortunately, visual learners do not usually have the same ease of language that auditory/verbal learners have and who would be better for sales than a person who had a great way with words? Clyde had dismantled his sales force who were good at thinking and speaking and making sales. Clyde got fired.

Auditory learners look to the left when they are accessing long term memory; which you would be doing in an interview when trying to recall the time of a successful selling event. Visual learners look to the upper right when recalling a visual event.

Kinesthetic learners, our athletic group of learners, look down to the right for skills, feelings and emotions and look down to the left to have an internal dialogue.

Staring straight ahead usually means no focus. Looking straight up means no emotion.

There is lots of meat in this bone for education. If you have a student who needs to calm down, have him look straight up. There is no emotion when you look up and the act will release the student from his emotions, outrage, anger or temper tantrum.

If you want to construct images, pictures or learn a mnemonic, look upper right and practice conjuring up a visual image. The information will be sent to short term memory. When you think you know it, look upper left and see if you can recall it. If you look up to the left and recall correctly, you have moved the information into long term memory which is where you look during a test.

If you want to remember definitions or words or mnemonics, look upper left and practice saying the definition or word. When you think you have it, look upper right and recall. If you recall, you have moved the information from short term memory to long term memory.

Think of where your student looks when caught doing something wrong and he is ashamed. When a student looks down to the right, it is usually where you look when you are in an ashamed state.

Today's students are more visual than auditory, what with TV, movies and You Tube. Long ago, the news came from the traveling minstrels who put the news to music and sang the news and families passed down their family stories by speaking.

Ask a person what he had for last night's dinner and watch the person's eyes. The person will search his long-term memory by looking up to the left where his visual memory is stored in his brain. He will see his last night's dinner scene or at least the food he ate.

If you see a student looking around with his eyes during a test, he may not be trying to look at another student's paper but shopping all through his brain looking for the answer; any answer.

Sight Readers

*I led the pigeons to the flag of the United States of America and to the public for Richard Stands one nation under guard And a vegetable with little tea and just rice for all. **(Unknown)***

At one time, in the history of education, sight reading was 'in' and phonics was 'out'. We have come full circle with phonics 'back in' as the primary strategy to teach reading and sight reading put out to pasture.

As a Learning Disability teacher, I knew both systems were to be used. It was never one way or the other. At Main Dunstable School and later in the Elementary Learning Center (ELC), I would test a student who had reading problems in class, to confirm whether or not the student was a sight reader. Phonics was a mystery and made for a miserable time in reading for every sight reader.

Some say, the student missed the important nuances in sounds as a toddler because of ear infections. For some it ran in the family. The gene pool was in effect from one generation to the next. No student uses just phonics or just sight words and needs both.

For the sight reader, I would dig out the Dolch List, make flash cards and practice with about 5 to 10 cards at a time. I would make piles of those mastered words and work on the remaining pile, increasing the mastered pile and decreasing the hit or miss pile. The cards were small and fitted into a student's pocket, so the student would take them home to practice with a pre-selected chosen member of the family.

The student and I would progress from a ten pack at a time and move on to an actual Dolch List and read from the list. Once the student had built up an inventory of memorized words, the teacher would say he was reading much better! Worked like a charm. The student didn't hear "Sound it out" from me.

Michi, my second grade Learning Disabled student with whom I worked for months on his sight words, made so much progress in reading in the classroom. His teacher told me that he was just immature - just delayed - and had simply matured. What do you say to that? I said "Probably so" out loud to the teacher.

While I was in the second grade and believing I was smart like my mother said, I was reading the Dick and Jane primer and worrying about having to read the whole page out loud; and we all know how short those pages were. Also, there was the matter of the workbooks that went along with the series. Every phonics page in my workbook had red marks all over the page and I had no clue why I'd got even one item wrong - let alone most of the page. Of course, I did not know how those numerous red marks had got all over my paper or what to do about it. I was supposed to be smart; I was told.

It all came clear to me after taking a phonics test in junior year of college at Keene State College during a methods course on how to teach reading. I failed. The test was a phonics test.

That's when the light came on in my head and knew I had never had any phonics sense – even then at my college age. I was a sight reader in a phonics world. The larger question loomed over me. How would I be able to teach phonics as a teacher if I had no clue to the phonics world? I carried my phonics book with me from one school assignment to another.

The light that came on gave me a reason for being a poor speller, too; but no solution. I remain a poor speller to this day. I never figured out the consistency in short vowel sounds. To compound the problem was my New England accent. I would also add an 'r' to some words and would leave it off other words. Even today I could still call myself Freider - not Freida - if I am not thinking. I still can't sound out the short vowels correctly and spell check was invented just for me. Up until the time I retired, I always kept a dictionary and thesaurus on my desk. Later, I found a digital spell checker left in a class. I was in heaven, and I admit I did not work hard to find the rightful owner.

Remember the classic line, "If you can't spell it, look it up in the dictionary." Well, one question that always came to mind was how? I usually gave up and used another word instead. Now I know enough to change the vowel to another one. "Look it up in the dictionary" should have been followed by "changing out the vowels." If it is not an 'o' then change it to another vowel - and so on - until you do find it in the dictionary.

Later in my life while contemplating a divorce, I put it off because who would spell for me and find my car keys? Now, I keep multiple car keys and use spell checker and oh, I did get the divorce.

Granddaughter Lily came along and guess what? Yes, she was a sight reader and on the verge of repeating first grade. I told her parents not to allow her to be held back. I would teach her to read over the summer.

As luck would have it, I got Lily and her sister Dawson for the summer. Dawson was a year older than Lily. Dawson had spent many a day reading to her class of peers from the teacher's reading chair, while repeating kindergarten because she was too young to enter first grade, according to Florida law.

Yes, her brain came equipped with a well-developed phonics disk. It was smooth sailing for her, but Lily tried to stay away from reading all summer long while I was trying in vain to fulfil the promise to her parents that Lily would be able to read on the second-grade level when she returned to school.

We were on our way to N.H. to stay on a lake with our friend, Ann. Lily filled our ears with crying in the car when I held up a flashcard.

While I got Lily sorted from her crying jag, Dawson got her own game going with Judy. Judy would see something out the window and have Dawson spell the word. I would have cried, too, if I had been Lily. Dawson was just too much for Lily.

Lily had a strong voice. No one could get away when she started one of her crying jags because we were trapped with her in the car. We did make it through the summer and Lily started second grade reading on grade level. I would call her in the evening and Lily would read her book to me over the phone. One night she called and read to me from her 'chapter' book. Yes, she made it to chapter books without pictures and today she has three bookcases in her bedroom filled with a collection of Anime books and beyond.

Lily became an 'A' student and was accepted into the International Baccalaureate program in high school, and she got straight 'A's in that program, too.

For want of a nail, the shoe was lost. For want of a shoe, the horse was lost. For want of a horse, the rider was lost. For want of a rider the battle was lost. For want of a battle, the kingdom was lost. And all for the want of a horseshoe nail. Ben Franklin is attributed to this quote, but it is a proverb said in different ways around the world. For want of the Dolch list, Lily was lost.

Work Smart not Hard.

*Life is a quick trip through time and space. **(Unknown)***

Sara McLoughlin says to me, "Raise your hand." "Why?" I ask. Sara says "to show you are interested". We are sitting in an Administration Masters level class at the University of Florida. I rack my brain to think of a question. I ask a harmless question and the professor answers "So far so good." The class is now half over, and Sara says, "Ask another question." and I repeat the process without asking why. Class is now over and Sara, who is in front of me, walks toward the professor instead of the door, introduces herself and begins a short chit chat with him. "What is she doing bothering him after class?" I think to myself. "He's probably annoyed and wants to get home" I think, but I hear myself joining in on the chit chat. We are now the last ones in the room. I think "He will know we are sucking up to him. We are losing his respect, and I am getting nervous". When we get out in the hall, I say, "What was that all about" but I am interrupted by Sara. She smiles and says, "That's how you get an 'A'." A light bulb went off in my mind. I needed to change my thinking. I didn't know you should chit chat with the teacher. Lesson learned. From there on, I followed all Sara's lessons on how to get an 'A'.

Sara says we should study together. Sara says, "He will ask this question. We practice putting together a paragraph that will answer the question and we rehearse what to say." Together we learn a pat answer for each question he might ask on the test. With the practice we put in, I could write out the paragraph that went with the question from memory. This is when another light bulb lit up. The professor only wants to hear his words coming back to him on a test. He does not want to hear my point of view. Parroting back the teacher's answer will get you an 'A'.

Sara showed me the power of mnemonics. We made up rhymes to remember the facts that Sara said would be asked on the final.

Later on, I take a final in another class, get outside and tell Sara I misread the question and answered something else.

Sara says, "Go back into the class and tell the professor what you told me. He will let you take back the test and let you fix it."

"I can't do that."

Sara says, "Go ahead, the worst he can do is say 'no'".

I say, "I can't do that.".

That is unheard of, I protest, but I give it a try. I told him I figured out the question while I was walking out. I answered the wrong question. The professor said sure. Here is your test. Of course, by now he knows me. He trusts me and gives me back my test. She is right, I make a new answer that answers the question. Sara's my wonderful "get an 'A' guru". I got an 'A' in every class I had with Sara. I would never doubt any of Sara's rules. I am learning how to chit chat with the professors, ask several questions in class - even if I already know the answer. Most importantly, I do not give my own opinion. It hinders your ability to get an 'A'!

Work Smart not Hard

Another reason why experience is the best teacher because she is always on the job. **(Unknown)**

Work smart not hard even though it is proper to say, "Work smarter not harder". I tell students to ask three questions in class, even though you do not know the answer. You can always say, "Please repeat the question" if you get called on and you do not know the answer. Lean forward when the teacher talks. Stare at some part of the face. This shows the teacher you are interested - even though you are just watching her wattle jiggle as she talks. Greet the teacher with a smile each time you enter the room and leave. Smile when the teacher says your name out loud while taking attendance. I explain that you want the teacher to think of you warmly. Build up your chits with the teacher so if a break can go your way, it will; because she has a warm fuzzy feeling about you and gives you the unexpected break you need. Sucking up to the teacher is good for you.

Of course, never turn in a paper without your name on it, and your name needs to be legible, too. I had heard of a teacher who humorously, but still scarily, took a paper without a name and ripped it up into little pieces in front of the class and threw it around the room as she ranted on about getting a paper to correct and not have the student's name on it. Her 'no name' problem was solved successfully.

Read the directions before beginning. There are several examples out there. One of the following directions tells the student to write their name and pass it to the teacher. Unfortunately, the directions to sign and pass in the paper was listed last.

While many of the other students are working on finishing the assignment and probably wondering how you got done so fast, you will become delighted to see lights go on with the students who read the directions. Have those students be quiet and let them watch the others work.

Chapter 9

Politics at Oviedo High

**Experience is what you get when you don't get your way.
(Unknown)**

I finally made it to high school! I developed a motivation program to sustain academic excellence. Joining me in recognizing the highest test grade for the week were the following businesses: Burger King, Pizza Hut, DQ and Dunkin Donuts. Each business gave coupons to me to be distributed to the student with the highest weekly test score. They also gave me coupons for my weekly review game, played every Friday after the test.

I was pleased to be accepted into the Seminole County Assistant Principal pool. In order to make exploring the world of car financing more interesting and motivating, I got the manager of Barnnet Bank to speak to my business/consumer math class about banking and buying a car. She insisted on a return visit and would bring individual print outs detailing the buyer's summary sheets.

I also got the name of the Junior Business League from the manager. I hoped to develop a joint program like many economics' classes have.

I also learned of a grant for building a smoother transition program between middle school and high school. I wrote the proposal requesting money to pay for substitutes to cover classes, while a team of Oviedo Learning Disabilities teachers worked on this program.

I made arrangements to provide CPR training for the emotionally handicapped students.

I developed a proposal between the Oviedo High School students and Lawton Elementary. My Emotionally Handicapped students would act as tutors for the younger student EH students.

I volunteered to coach the girls' tennis next year.

I volunteered to write grants with the Learning Disabilities team teachers.

I signed up for two courses required for EH certification to better fulfill my teaching assignment as I was teaching one class of Emotionally Handicapped students for which I was not certified.

I was selected to attend the David Lane's summer seminar.

I got travel companies to give me colorful posters to hang on my windowless room.

I got two unused apple computers for my classroom along with two boxes of free math disks for my students to use.

I took a graduate course in supervision so I could be part of the University of Central Florida's Student Teacher Program.

I completed the required number of hours in ESOL training.

I was selected to be a presenter at the Council for Exceptional Children Florida's Federation Annual Conference. My topic was Motivation: the forgotten Resource for a Safer School Environment.

I was selected to participate in the Florida Humanities Council's Summer Seminar.

Through the Center for Creatively, Innovations and Leadership, I was selected to participate in the Citizen Ambassador Program of People to People International. I would be the co-leader of the Woman in Education contingent which would be meeting with women at the highest levels in education, business and government throughout China.

In the school year, I was given a teaching assignment consisting of four classes, grades and emotional levels. During the year, I saw students going from automatically putting 'F' at the top of their papers to feeling they could pass or make a better grade. I saw students who started class trying to cheat at every chance turning into students who found they could do the work and not have to cheat.

I took classes where students called each other names and made fun of others and turned them into classes of students who helped each other. I was able to achieve the best. My students were learning and helping each other learn and they felt good about it. Learning in many areas was taking place. Anyone can stand in front of the class and do problems on the overhead. I taught my students how to learn. A pretty good year, I thought. I was not nominated for re-hire. On my last evaluation, I received "needs improvement".

I later learned that my principal was good friends with Beth P. and they had attended training together in Arizona. Politics had arrived, yet again.

Chapter 10

Andros Island Became My Vacation

Patience my ass. I am going to kill something. (Unknown)

I went from teaching at a high school to teaching 7 students on Andros Island in the Bahamas.

Being on an island meant the kids you went to school with were also the same ones you played with outside of school. If you got mad at your friend at school, with whom would you hang around with outside of school?

Sounds easy: only 8 students. In reality, I had a class of special needs students. Elaina, Brian, Halsey, Dane, Alan, Sharon, Kirsten and Molly. Alan was the tallest child who cried at unexpected times. Sharon was learning disabled. Dane was an introvert and a day dreamer. He lived in the world of boats. Halsey was named after a boat and could catch any critter, especially snakes. Brian was the supporter, trying to be everyone's friend and peace maker. Elaina was quiet, smart, tiny and introverted. Kirsten was a fourth-grade oceanographer in the making. Molly filled the whole room with her presence, loud and insistent on a lot of attention. She was an agitator, as well.

Something needed to change. They were not likable. How will I change the students from constantly bickering like siblings into an enjoyable class? Molly was going to give me a run for my money. She sucked the air out of the room and put her needs first. I had a year contract on this island.

Well, as luck would have it, Molly, who kept things stirred up, moved off the island. My work was cut out for me - even without Molly in the mix. A Montessori quote came to mind. "The first thing to be done, therefore, is to discover the true nature of a child and then assist him in his normal development." (Montessori)

Somewhere along the way, Alan learned he was of value; that the students respected his drawing skills which he didn't know he had. He lost the need to cry. Brian learned he had so many helping skills, he smoothly transitioned from "Let me help" to "Let me lead". He became the accepted leader of our merry little group. One time, he took over the lesson and taught a concept in math for Sharon, who could hear his explanation and not mine - no matter how many ways I tried to explain.

He said, "Let me try." He did and Sharon got "it" which delighted Brian and me and Sharon, as well.

Dane began to accept that school was there, daily, to help train his brain so he could make a living in his world of boats. I don't think he really bought the whole package, but he learned to save his daydreaming to outside of class. Halsey was our happy-go-lucky naturalist. The time was 'before the internet' and we did not have a library, so he was a self-taught naturalist.

We got Elaina, tiny and quiet, to star in our Christmas play. She was going to be our live Christmas tree angel on the top of the Christmas tree. Unfortunately, she froze during the final scene. I climbed the ladder and walked her off the stage. Alan came through by picking up the lines and finishing the play. She never gave me a reason for her freezing up, but she did come out and take a final bow with the rest of her class. Kirsten was the most 'normal' student. She brought her happy personality to class each day, worked independently, and showed me the hidden world of tiny critters in the tidal pools along the beach. She was my one teacher-independent student.

I only got a year on another dream job. A new contractor came in to run the base and I was the last hired and the first fired.

Chapter 11

Politics at Challenger 7 Elementary School

The greatest sign of success for a teacher...is to be able to say, the children are now working as if I did not exist.
(Maria Montessori)

So, there I am at Challenger 7 Elementary School for the first time, substituting in a class where the students work on their own without the teacher directing the activity, which happened to be reading. Let me elaborate. My next-door teacher partner came in to say that the kids knew what to do and I didn't have any direct instruction responsibilities. Because I did not have anything to prep before class started, I spread out a newspaper found on a desk in the room and looked through the newspaper to entertain myself but mostly to pass time.

The class sounded like the Montessori quote "The greatest sign of success for a teacher...is to be able to say, "The children are now working as if I did not exist."" (Montessori.) Well, in came the kids and they started working. I walked around the room asking the kids what they were doing and offering my help, if needed. The students were able to tell me what they were doing and after a sweep of the room, I agreed the students were working on their own. I was so proud of the teacher. I wanted to meet her. It sounded to me that I would want to teach at this school.

As it turned out, the paper spread out on a desk, was a red flag. I got a note at the end of the day from the principal saying I would not be asked back to substitute because all I did was sit at my desk and read the paper.

The assistant principal had come in the room while I was not at the desk where the paper was spread out. She asked me how it was going, and I told her it was going well, that the students knew what they were doing. She left.

After I heard the feedback from the principal, I could not help but feel sorry for that amazing teacher and sad that this school was not for me; but glad to know I would not be happy working there.

Chapter 12

Montessori Greeting

What is a weed? A plant whose virtues have not yet been discovered. (Unknown)

I got to work at Montessori School after being fired from Oviedo High. It didn't pay the bills, but I got to rest for a while.

The students come in from their cars through the entrance of the building and into the middle of the open room. Each student follows the same procedure, puts away lunch, takes off their sweater and sits cross legged on the large circle, neither causing an uproar nor having simple negative interactions among themselves and besides, it was early morning. I figured, this alone time in the big circle was a worthy transitioning from the hectic morning routine at the start of school.

The Montessori Director goes through her morning procedure. She has each student share Show and Tell, daily calendar, weather report and greets each student individually with a handshake and says something positive to each student and, of course, the smile. At this point the students leave to go to their individual classrooms.

I remember a similar procedure when I was in school, I was bored and felt like it was a waste of time. I still don't pay much attention to the date and the weather, to my detriment, but the morning circle routine is necessary for the verbal extrovert personality.

The extrovert verbal student needs the early morning interaction in a controlled setting. The extrovert learns patience, impulse control and that delay of gratification or recognition which will serve the student well in future years because the circle teaches teacher-pleasing behaviors.

The introvert, on the other hand, needs to learn social interaction skills and learn the importance of the calendar and weather daily. It is a life skill that I still have not mastered. I remember a story from Cousin Diane. She brought home a survey paper that she had filled out in class. She remembers her mother looking at a one of her fourth-grade papers and asking. "What do you mean you don't know in what month your birthday is?" or "Which month is Christmas in?" "Why do you think your kidneys are in your head?" (She is a very talented creative person in real life.)

When you come across a well-run, happy class; know that early morning procedures/class rituals are aplenty, with more rituals happening throughout the day: such as watering the plants, caring for the class pet, cleaning up, clapping the erasers, washing the board, visiting guests and lining up, etc. Rituals are the glue that binds the students together into a sense of belonging for 180 school days.

Chapter 13

Reading is Harder Now.

Anytime you see a turtle up on top of a fence post, you know he had some help. (unknown)

1. Literate high school grads. need to know 60,000 words.

2. Average students enter high school with only 5,000. They need to learn 4,000 words a year or 70 new words a week.

3. The best strategy for learning this number of words is to read a large amount of narrative and informational text. That is about 25-35 books a year. Another way to look at it is about a million to a million and a half words of running text from late first grade onwards.

4. In fourth and fifth grades, one million words of running text contain 40,000 words which will appear only once or twice, yet are crucial to the passage meaning.

5. Out of 40,000 students will learn 2000 – 3000 of these words by learning them in context.

6. From decoding to storage and immediate retrieval of a word, the word needs to be read successfully 4 – 14 times. Gifted students only need one or a couple of times reading a word successfully, while Learning disabled students may need 14 times.

7. Students must learn 3000 to 4000 a year to stay on grade level.

8. Students need to spend at least an hour a day reading.

9. As textbooks get larger and more difficult, teachers seem to be avoiding reading in social studies, science and math.

10. Students must be taught how to read difficult vocabulary, how to interpret the increasing number of visuals in textbooks - colorful charts, graphics or maps, the inclusion of which has been driven by a pervasive, image-oriented, electronics-based, popular media.

11. Textbooks are losing ground to other media - CD-roms, videos or hands on projects.

12. Reading textbooks has joined the stand-by of chalk board.

13. In 1998, 26% of 8th graders and 23% of high school students were below grade level. (NEAP)

14. In some inner-city schools, 80% can fail to meet grade level reading standards.

15. The number one problem is reading comprehension: Lack of comprehension is caused by lack of fluency, limited vocabulary or background knowledge, or minimal interest.

16. Secondary teachers feel they lack expertise in teaching so that fact lets them off the hook.

17. Lecture – Most girls like 200 words per minute. Boys like slightly less. 150 words per minute is best for comprehension.

18. Establishing a community of readers is the initial goal of Academic Literacy.

The above stats are dated but the results are likely to be worse today (post covid time frame). I don't remember where I got this information, so I cannot give credit. I may have taken the information from multiple studies. I apologize for the lazy excuse.

I do want to clarify the term 'inner city schools'. There is a flip side to this phrase. There have been (and presently are) many inner-city schools that produce successful citizens and college degree student. Inner city schools are a stereotype of the big picture. These successful schools quietly go about educating and only get mentioned when a movie is made about one of them. It would be a game changer if the 'inner city schools' reached out and discovered what makes a successful school. There are successful models out there that have programs that can be replicated in schools of need elsewhere.

Beat the Clock Reading List Competition

School teachers are not fully appreciated by parents until it rains all day Saturday. **(Unknown)**

While teaching reading to ninth graders at Titusville High School, I learned how many words students need to know to be on grade level and I started Reading List Completion after a pre-game practice time. A student would volunteer to read a column from lists that we had been practicing while going against the clock. The next volunteer would repeat the game, trying to beat the other student's time, his previous time, and of course, they may end up with the best time in the class for that trial.

All the students had a copy of the word list and would read along to themselves during the competition while attempting to keep up with the contestant. (They were the judges on correct pronunciation.)

Pause to remember that a student has three vocabulary levels. One level defines the difference between using a word verbally and using it in the written form. Sometimes we see a word in print that we have used numerous times verbally but have not seen it in print- a pleasant surprise and a chance to make a new connection.

Our verbal vocabulary is larger than our written vocabulary: So, this exercise helps a student see in print a word that the student had been using, sometimes for years, but had not used in written language.

For example: Carousel - often called a merry-go-round: I had ridden on them over the years and finally decided to look it up in the dictionary. I did not stay the course. I gave up searching for it in the dictionary and in my writing, I used the phrase "merry-go-around" instead. There was only so much frustration I could tolerate, so I accepted failure and moved on. Those like me, repeat our mantra. "How can you look up a word in the dictionary if you don't know how to spell it." Remember when you asked how to spell a word, only to be told to look it up in a dictionary. Useless information. Why didn't the teachers tell me to change out the vowels? I usually drifted off looking at different words and forgot what word I was looking for in the dictionary in the first place.

The third level is the word you hear in your head but may not know how to spell or pronounce out loud in conversation because you are not sure of the pronunciation. Back in those days it offered an easy opportunity for a student to laugh at another student's inadequacy. Very few students had the ability to resist doing this. I certainly was not brave enough to read the word out loud to the class and risk mockery.

In my class the pre-game practice was actually a fun time. Each student would turn to a partner to practice reading the column. Each student was expected to ask for correct pronunciation and welcome corrections on pronunciation. After all, it was only practice, you were with a friend, and you were free to speak out loud in class.

There are numerous lists for each grade level. There are word lists to describe students, words they are likely to encounter on high stakes tests, lists by theme, alphabetical word lists, student-specific lists, synonyms, antonyms, FRY sight word lists, and even word list templates, basic reading inventory lists and of course, student-generated lists.

While teaching in the Elementary Learning Center (ELC) center at Frankfurt International School in Germany (FIS), I had a button machine. Each student got a badge with the work of the day. The ticket system gave the student a ticket for each time the student used the word in their class and at home. To record, the student put a tick mark on the back of the button. I counted the tick marks and gave a student a ticket for each tick mark. It was not important how many tickets each student earned. It was important to try out using a new word. We gave many tickets for any step toward practicing a good habit. The store was expensive, as well.

What I learned was my classes had many more students of phonics than sight readers. I never had a non-reader in any of my reading classes, regardless of the grade level. However, I did meet way too many students who had no time for reading.

Reading had fallen out of favor sometime after Dick and Jane and before Joe Mini Goats in fourth grade. I had the honor of taking ninth grade students to the library. They said that they had never been in one before - at least in their own mind. Many elementary schools had a library visit once a week. I should have left that out so it would have sounded better for me, but I like moderation in my exaggeration.

I had the great opportunity to be walking by a student who was finishing up his book, a ninth grader who had already reached his full growth. He paused when I got into his peripheral view, looked at me, smiled and said with a grin on his face, "I never finished a book before. IT WAS PRETTY GOOD."

Boring Reading has a Learning Curve

The natural state of a human being is to be happy, full of life and interest and curiosity. ***(Earl Nightingale)***

I called incomprehensible reading "Boring Reading." I would read short (very short in the beginning) articles on my interest level. The student's goal was to make it to the end of my boring reading. I would then ask who stayed on the course all the way through.

With a show of hands, we would learn who got better at trying to stay focused. As expected, as I began this habit, most hands went up when I asked who "tuned out" in the beginning. There was no grade on comprehension, but over time more and more accepted the challenge to try to stay tuned in. Peer pressure.

On some later occasions of Boring Reading, I would get some hands up of those who made it to the end. It was few. Most students improved the habit by making it to the level of tuning in and out or at least making it further than they had before and not without hearing the amazement in their voice when they spoke of their results. Most were amazed that they had found themselves listening to any of the Boring Reading at all.

It was not the comprehension I measured but the improvement in the habit of staying tuned in when the teacher was speaking; however, boring the teacher's words were to the student who was supposed to be listening.

Transitions Lead the Way

*In matters of style, swim with the current: In matters of principle, stand like a rock. **(Unknown)***

There are many words used to transition but generally 6 categories. Check them out with a search, (eg. https://www.insegnanti-inglese.com/grammar-1/conjunctions-transitions.html).

They are words or phrases to help sequence ideas (or transitions) between sentences or paragraphs. Transition words are the road signs in writing. They help readers follow your train of thought without becoming bogged down trying to discern your meaning. When used correctly, they keep up the flow of your writing as you shift in meaning, tone and ideas from one sentence or paragraph to another. I learned of transitions at a workshop taken after earning my master's degree.

The above definition may certainly have come in handy as I sat in my second-grade seat with a clean piece of special short composition paper. The class assignment was to write something. With the transition sheet, I at least could have started a few sentences. Instead, I sat there at my little desk and demanded a thought come to me. Nothing did and I never did put anything on that special white composition paper. In hindsight, the white composition paper should have been used as a final copy.

While teaching at Memorial Middle School in Orlando, I had the students write and rewrite the same essay all week. The grade would be given on Friday after four rewrites. I called it 'editing'. The goal was for the students to turn in a finished product on Friday. I never did advance to the creative process. Instead, I would acknowledge students on Monday who turned in the cleanest copy on the preceding Friday. The class was working on the mechanics of writing. This is the same group who refused to receive their textbook which was the traditional English Comp book of the day, smaller than the average size with a blue and white cover called 'English Comp'. I remember passing them out while the students were returning the books to me and not in a polite way, either. Some were yelling out "I can't read." The class as a whole told me where they were in the education process, and it wasn't seventh grade composition.

I had just returned from teaching at the Frankfurt International School, my teaching utopia, to learn that a whole class of 30 learning disabled student had all slipped through the same crack. Think of it - the middle school was fed students from various elementary schools: enough elementary schools to create a whole class of 30 Learning Disabled seventh grade students. While I was on my Memorial Middle School assignment, I was in my learning strategies class - held in the old chemistry equipment closet. I heard the word "fight" and a commotion in the hall. Someone had yelled "fight" during the changeover between classes and the whole wing emptied out the side door to see the fight. The other learning-disabled teacher, Cathy, told me she went out in the hall to stop the throng of running students and got knocked over.

I had the same group of students in my history class as I had in seventh grade English Comp. Again, we practiced writing the answer as a complete sentence with correct spelling in their history workbooks. We did not use an actual history book. I had learned my lesson. The students had already spoken loud and clear to me about what they thought of our textbooks. I became a talking dictionary - spelling out words for them. No, I did not make them look the words up in a dictionary. There were none in the room anyway. Our 'transitions' consisted of picking a word from the preceding sentence to link our sentences together. The students were graded on how well they wrote the joint answer. I called the strategy 'the train'. Connect the next sentence to the previous sentence using a word from the previous sentence to link the thoughts together.

I would have stayed at this school assignment but the principal who hired me was moving on. The new principal described herself as a 'fisher woman' who took a book instead of a fishing pole. According to my four personality groups the principal was a C personality. She was big on dotting the 'I's and crossing the T's. I did not see any support for my program and changed school assignments. The present principal was promoted to the county office. He escaped and so did I.

Teacher: Read Aloud and Get the Silence you Deserve

Even when freshly washed and relieved of all obvious confections, children tend to be sticky. ***(Fran Lebowitz)***

What is the best intervention for a restless class? We have story time in the primary years, and we should continue through high school. When I taught sixth grade in Dover, N. H., I read out loud to the class about those restless moments when the students signaled that a break time was needed and I wished to re-focus them.

I added "doodle time" to my oral reading sessions which consisted of scrap paper for students who wished to draw as they listened. Idle hands were busy and quiet.

I explained about a doodle lady who doodled and how her doodles became a money-maker for her. She sold her doodles to a puzzle maker who happened to be the father of her roommate in college. Her doodles paid her way through college. I told them, I was sure Charlie Brown started out as a Charles Schultz doodle in some elementary school somewhere.

In addition to listening, I engaged their eyes and hands, as well. Engage three senses and you might have three chances to captivate the whole class and re-focus their attention.

Before my time as a teacher, I was read to as a high school student by the teacher. Mr. White read us a book in my sophomore year. I remember asking myself, "Why?" There were no tests or discussions from day to day. He had probably already tried to have each student read during the literature class over the years and figured he may just as well read it to us. He was a gray haired, balding, older man who wore glasses, had one bulging eye, crooked teeth and a crooked smile. Some of us might have received some of his spittle from time to time as he read. He was in fact the only English teacher I remembered from high school, and I still remember the 'Tale of Two Cities'.

As time went on, I added costume to my oral reading to students. I read Edgar Allan Poe in my black robe and one candle in the room for light. (Against the fire code.)

I do not remember a teacher reading to us in my elementary years, but I remember students had to read out loud - one after another, row by row - in my classes. It was too stressful for me. I feared I would lose my place and mispronounce words: besides, my palms sweated profusely. I figured reading out loud was more of a performance and decided from then on, that practice was needed Even our plays were practiced first.

Success is Built from Tiny Steps.

Experience may be a thorough teacher, but no person lives long enough to graduate. ***(Unknown)***

The buzz word 'scaffolding' entered the teaching lexicon and was very annoying to me because, as the teacher, I became responsible if the student did not learn. The scaffolding was meant to break down the skill into tiny steps that the student could master, enabling him/her to move on to the next step toward successfully mastering the skill. The concept was taken from the field of Learning Disabilities.

The problem arose when educators tried to apply the technique to all students. The name 'scaffolding' was born and immediately ruined when trying to apply it to all students because teachers outside of the Learning Disabilities didn't know what it meant and how to apply it; but they knew they were being held accountable for their student's lack of success. To teachers it meant making it easier for the student and just like that, education went back to 10 spelling words instead of 20 for some students which was the solution back in 1967 when I started teaching.

We have come full circle. Toward the end of my teaching career in 2012, I had to read the whole standardized test (called FCAT in Florida) out loud to a third-grade autistic student. The student ignored me and colored in the circle of each answer before I finished reading the question while standing up (which he was allowed to do in the classroom). He rarely sat during the day. On the second day of me reading the exam to him, he came in the room and began pacing the room while muttering to himself, "F**king FCAT."

Around the same time, I filled in for another teacher and worked with Robert with his reading. While walking the student back to his room, he asked, "Why didn't you say "good job" and other nice things to me like the other teacher does?"

I said, "Because you didn't try to work hard. You did not do a nice job today."

There is always room for a reality check when working with students who have been filled with false hope and an inflated sense of themselves. And that dumb idea came out of the Middle School concept where the first job of the teacher became making students feel good about themselves - even in failure. At college they now need safe spaces and certain groups excluding others from joining their clubs.

Reluctant Reader

*For those who understand, no explanation is needed. For those who do not understand no explanation is possible. **(Unknown)***

A teacher before me at THS got a grant for paperback books. It was the best-stocked class library - especially for a reading class in high school. Too many librarians did not want "them" in the library because they were not interested in reading and would fool around and get books out of order.

Wouldn't you like to have students come to class knowing that each got to take a break from the daily class routine? I learned how to create a self-starting class of ninth graders who had to take this class until they passed the state mandated test. They had to enter, sit down, get out a book that they had been carrying around and read while I took attendance. Silent reading for the reluctant reader began when the students entered the class, so it was a self-starting class. While I took attendance, I also assessed the class to find out who had immediate needs that needed attention.

The process went as follows:

Step 1. A student picks a book.

Step 2. If you do not like the book, put it back and get another book.

Step 3. When you finish, get another book.

Even I am in disbelief as I read this. What's the catch? How did I get a class of 25 ninth and tenth grade students who hated reading to sit quietly and read a book in class?

I started with the belief that ninth and 10th graders could read. I had taught long enough on the elementary level, regular education and in Learning Disabilities to make that assumption. The problem these students had was that they didn't like to read, and some could not score well on a reading test, either. A double whammy needed to be overcome in reading.

Playing in the background was "Pachelbel's Canon in D major" also known as 'Canon'. A German Baroque composer Johann Pachelbel composed it. The important part of the music is the 60 beats per minute. Research has pointed out that 60 beats per minute releases alpha waves. (See Silva Method) Alpha waves relax the mind and concentration is improved. The students bought into the routine, and I would have a really silent reading period. The only movement heard in the room would be from a student who was exchanging a book.

Silent reading procedure had a learning curve - a steep learning curve for some. The procedure for silent reading had to be practiced by some more than others; but they all got there.

In the beginning, most students grabbed any book and took it back to their seats. Some students held their books upside down. Some students held their book up in front of their mouth while speaking to a neighbor. Some students never turned the page. Some students had the book open while daydreaming and looking elsewhere in the room.

When I saw avoidance tactics, I would ask the student if he/she liked the book The student always said "no" and I sent them back to our in-class library to get another book. My response was to point out to the student that he needed to return the book and get another one. No one was in trouble and the student accepted he was called out and acknowledged the call out with a smile that said he/she was" busted" by the teacher.

When a student finally finds a book that keeps his/her attention he/she will finish it. Just don't count the number of times he/she changes the book. This is where the teacher's observation pays off.

Also in the beginning, I would fix the loop-holes the students would use to get out of reading quietly and alone for pleasure. At the end of class, I would do a teacher check to make sure the book was in their book bag or in their back pocket. There was a detention for anyone who left their book at home and one for leaving the book behind at the end of class. For a few students the silent reading book was the only thing in their book bag. We had a practice period before detentions were issued and I don't remember giving out any detentions. It was an easy procedure to buy into.

I would bring up a situation a lot where they might be bored while riding in the car, waiting in lines, being sent to their room at home. Pulling out the book from the book bag could be a life savior. No one was assigned pages to read daily, either.

Many reading teachers love to recommend a book for a student but what do they really know about the student's interest on the high school level? No student wanted to spend time telling the teacher his interests. Students probably didn't know their interests, because they hate reading and besides, their only interest at this stage in life was social.

I made a presentation to a reading conference about my silent reading program for the reluctant reader and received applause from fellow teachers; but nothing came of it. I wondered if it was the fact that I was one hundred and eighty degrees from the thinking of the traditional reading teachers who were an influential part of the conference. Be it an English teacher or even the librarian, the questions would have been the same. Where is accountability? How do you know he understood the book? What was the theme? How do you know the student read it? What will the parents say? "Where's your proof?" was my favorite question.

The proof is in front of us. No adult takes a quiz on a fiction book from the best seller list. Who would give the quiz? We read for pleasure. That is the pleasure of reading fiction! It is the pleasure part of reading in school. The goal is to get the students to go faithfully to the library as adults and remain lifelong learners. Why take the pleasure out of reading in the one area of a reading program that is supposed to be fun? Move the plot, theme, etc. into its own section of the reading program every day. My program had no external rewards. The reward was the enjoyment of living vicariously through others' lives in a book.

The test results from our required state testing were announced by Dr. Christy, the principal, at the faculty meeting at the beginning of my second year. The low scoring students?? increased by 7 percentage points which he was amazed and happy to report.

Hot Microphone

It is extremely difficult to lead further than you have gone yourself.
(Unknown)

I bought a microphone with a grant I received. It changed my thinking and made me a better teacher. With the mike, I could hear myself speaking. It was as if I was listening to my words from the students' point of view. I now paid attention to my own words. This caused me to express myself more clearly, use better choices of words and not to ramble on and repeat myself. It is said that teachers use the same 17 words each week, consisting mainly of commands.

There are some students who, after years of training, shut down as soon as the teacher begins the lecture. Over the years, some students have become annoyed by the often-repeated phases such as "you know", "Okay", "Like", "Right?", "Mmm" and the rest of phrases spoken to fill in the void while you are thinking on your feet.

The mike can also be used to quieten a student down by simply quietly walking by a talking student and putting the mike up to someone you wish to be quiet.

Bulletin Board for 'A' Papers.

My dog is so lazy, he won't bark when a rabbit runs by. He waits until the neighbor's dog barks. Then he just nods his head. **(Unknown)**

While teaching math at Oviedo High I set up a bulletin board for 'A' papers after I witnessed students just tossing their returned work into the trash. I said to remember back to the days when you were proud to have papers up on the refrigerator door; the family bulletin board. I explained that I was replacing the family fridge with an 'A' paper board. I had to ask for the 'A' paper at first and proudly stapled the paper to the board. They made the most out of stapling their 'A' paper to the 'A' paper board in a line. Some of the students created a scene stapling their papers to the board, adding several staples; some were verbal about the 'A' all the way to the board. Some just beamed.

At the end of the semester, students' 'A' papers were removed from the board, counted and passed back to the students. Some left the room with their papers. Some said, "I do not need these anymore". Some got their papers all the way home.

Movie Time Is Great for Finding and Learning literature Terms

There are two educations. One should teach us how to make a living and the other how to live. **(Unknown)**

Showing movies is a sticky wicket in the area of education. Too many bureaucrats believe showing a movie to a class means loss of teaching time, a waste of learning time, a teacher just slacking off the job, etc, but how about offering real stories in the form of a movie with an assignment. This is what the students taught me.

Plot - It has been said if you are pitching a new project in the movie industry you get five minutes and must tell the whole story condensed into three sentences. Have the students learn that the plot is the thread of the story, and it has a beginning, middle and the end.

Have students write down a few sentences from the beginning, middle and end of the movie. When it is read by the teacher it becomes a shortened down plot and more like a summary. It must make sense as a shortened story. When a student demonstrates mastery of the plot, the student is set free and no longer required to write out the plot. The student simply watches for enjoyment.

Theme – Explain that the theme can be said in many ways. It represents why the person wrote the story in the first place. Have the student write out the theme at the end of the movie. It can be a single word or a phrase. When a student demonstrates mastering the theme, the student simply enjoys the movie.

Climax – Have students look for the last moment before the story ties up loose ends. The climax is the last suspense for the reader. It is just before all is answered for the reader.

Use the same format for other literary terms that you want the students to practice learning such as main character and the problem to be overcome by the main character made into a hero. Depending on the class, Students may work on more than one literary term per movie.

Books on Tape

Nothing lasts forever. Not even your troubles. **(Unknown)**

I don't remember the program's name, but it must have been quite expensive. I had the students pick a fiction book, get the matching tape, recorder, earphones, read and take the test.

It created problems that I was not able to solve. One: Was the tape on? Two: Is it a school tape? At the end there was a test on the computer for the students to take. Three: What do I do with that grade?

Do you want to put up with the assistant principal quietly coming in to bust a student with ear buds and disrupting our quiet self-starting class? I retired from the program before I started a health concern with the sharing of the ear buds. I did offer to any interested student the book and tape to try at home. I got very few takers: actually none.

There is More than One Reading Rate

The business of a teacher is to turn obstacles into stepping-stones, weakness into success and disaster into triumph. **(Unknown)**

My reluctant reading students believed if they did not read fast, they would be poor readers. Their silent reading in the beginning of class at Titusville High was reading for enjoyment. The book should be easy to read. If you find yourself reading too slowly in silent reading, put the book back and get another one. If you missed not being able to pronounce and/or know the meaning of a word 5 times on one page, put the book back and get another one.

One student taught me this. She always reads the end of a book. If she liked it, she would try out the book. If she didn't like the ending, *she would get another book.*

And I thought there was some rule against reading the ending before the beginning.

My 'boring reading' exercise was read by me in a moderate to slow speed; emphasizing, pausing at the end of sentences and after some words. reading groups of words as common phrases they may have in their listening voice. (I'm not sure what you mean here.)

The non-fiction books for oral book reports that the students got from the library were dependent on subject level interest, rather than easy or hard to read. I explained about picture books for grownups; that 'reading' pictures was a reading skill. Convincing students that picture books for adults were reading, too, I explained it was all right to read captions only. I explained it was okay to thumb through the non-fiction book only reading what caught their eye.

In my own case, when I tried to read my textbooks in college, I fell asleep constantly. When I took notes, I spent most of my time trying to figure out how to spell a word so that I would lose the point or gist of what the lecturer was saying.

It was finally, after college, that I learned to just listen in a relaxed state of mind.

I read my first magazine after college. It was "Newsweek". I was astounded at how many words I had to skip because I could not pronounce them or did not know the meaning. It was slow going. There was a lot of re-reading: as though I were reading about dark holes for the first time. There must be a way to sound out long words. My reading rate was turtle speed. There was phonics rearing its ugly head again in my life.

While living in Ithaca, N.Y., I took a course on children's lit. There I found my easy reading rate. It had been amazing to experience living vicariously through the printed text. I finely got it. I was reading for pleasure, so I read over 100 adolescent books for that course. My favorite book from that experience was "A Wrinkle in Time." by Madeleine L'Engle.

Do you want to put up with the assistant principal quietly coming in to bust a student with ear buds and disrupting our quiet self-starting class? I retired from the program before I started a health concern with the sharing of the ear buds.

I did offer to any interested student the book and tape to try at home. I got very few takers, actually, none.

During this time, I learned about the New York Times best seller list and kept up the top ten in fiction for years. Years later, I graduated to non-fiction books, including financial and political. By now I had found a way to sound out long words. Yeah, for me.

Later on, I would read the first sentence of a paragraph in a book of fiction and keep a running gist of the story. I scanned the descriptive paragraphs sketching a scene in my mind. I was speed reading and finally ahead of the curve in reading in my mind.

"We are the Champions"

Nothing is more common than unsuccessful men with talent.
(Calvin Coolidge)

My favorite ritual is passing back the quiz or test - mostly quizzes. This happens quite a lot. The more feedback over short periods of time, the better. To set the scene, cue the music: "We Are the Champions" by Freddy Mercury and Queen is now playing on the CD. As the song plays in the background, I bring out the stack of papers already in descending order. The 'A' papers are first to be given out. I call out an 'A' student's name, smile and hand the student the 'A' paper. While I am giving out the papers, I sometimes hear my favorite line which, when I hear it, is feedback to me. My favorite line is hearing a random student yell after I called a particular student's name, "HE, got an 'A'? Him?" I stop to smile again at the student who just got the 'A' and he smiles back.

This is what I hear in my mind. It is feedback to me from the class. I hear instead, "Oh, if he can get an 'A', I should be able to get one, too."

My 'A' paper student even got a shout of esteem from his peers. I remember thinking how nice it was to have him on my train all week, too. I also know that if he got an 'A' this week, he could do it next week and I would use this to motivate him during the next week.

There is a wealth of insight in this event, where he feels the reward for effort as well as working on his new good habit. The next day, I would be able to point out the good feeling he got with his 'A'. I would ask what he had done differently last week to get an 'A'. Once he verbalizes what he did differently, I would file it away to the tip of my tongue to be used for reminders during the next week as he practices his new habit and gets to repeat his success of last week.

If the student changes one habit and gets the intended result, he/she will be more receptive to practicing another new habit that he/she needs to build on his small success. And of course, I say, "It takes 21 days to learn a new habit and most people give up on day 17." and give him a new habit to practice.

It takes 21 days to learn a new habit and most give up on day 17. Whether it holds up to scientific experiment is not the point, is it? Persistence in error is a sign of a fool. I ask if he knows he is not getting the desired results, it is time to change your plan. Step one 1. Name the problem. 2. Why it is a problem? 3. Have the student suggest several choices of what might work. 4. Decide on a plan. 5. Practice, practice, practice. 6. Give yourself feedback and reshape the plan as needed.

The idea behind day 17 may be just a marker to shoot for, light at the end of the tunnel, or maybe the power of thought.

Here is the hard part. It is important to remember who is practicing what habit, notice when the habit is being practiced, and give the student sincere feedback such as: "I like it when you read to yourself", "Your handwriting is looking neater", "You raised your hand", "You stayed in your seat the whole class", "I only reminded you to get back to work three times this class", "That's your best record", "That was nice of you to do that", "Thanks for helping Derik", "You remembered your own pencil, today", "I like it when you raise your hand". "Is it getting easier?" and on and on.

If you hear a sports analogy being used, you are right. A coach sees a skill the player needs, points it out and encourages the student to practice. More coaches than not compliment the player when he performs the skill well and encourages the student to keep working on the skill and later, related skills. Many skills can be practiced on the field and off.

Scholastic Magazine Plays are a Hidden Gem.

*When the best leaders work is done, the people say, we did it ourselves. (**Unknown**)*

Scholastic Magazine included a short play in each monthly magazine. Why not read the play in class, I asked myself. Would they think it was beyond them at this age?

From my own experience in eighth grade, I remember having to read out loud for the whole class to hear. "Oh, no I used to think "She is in my row, I am going to be next," - sweaty palms and a knot in my stomach.

"What if I can't pronounce a word or lost my place?" I wasn't listening to the material as the others took turns reading before me. I called up my bad habit instead. I didn't listen to the others read out loud after me. I was too busy analyzing how poorly my oral reading went. I am supposed to be smart. What's wrong with me?

I had developed the poor habit of self-applied fear while oral reading in my daily reading group in second grade. The fear was still with me in the eighth grade.

"Oh, no, I am next." I would worry and was self-analyzing my mistakes. There were probably only four words on a page, but monumental to me.

If the teacher had to help me while I read, I had failed before my teacher and peers. The whole process was compounded by being in the top reading group. After all, I was supposed to be smart. What was wrong with me?

Well, we tried reading the play out loud and the results were way beyond my expectations. Twenty-five ninth and tenth graders in a remedial reading class would stand up, read the monthly play without losing their place, without stammering over words and several would even read with expression, as well.

At this point, you are wondering, what was the catch? How long did it take to organize and get through three plays? How did we get through the ordeal? Maybe you wondered what I glossed over?

Here is how it looks. Three captains were chosen by me. Sometimes I chose 3 "popular" students, sometimes 3 "quiet" students and sometimes three students who needed some attention.

All three captains started by picking their friend, then those two would get together to pick the next addition to their team. The students were trained to pick teams from their "Heads Up" days in elementary school and it would go smoothly each time. "Heads Up" was a game to settle down a class and considered to be a waste of time in elementary years. Seven students secretly tap seven other students who have their heads down. Someone yells "heads up" so the tapped students stand and guess who tapped him or her.

When we had enough students to cover the parts, the rest became judges and worked with me. There were usually three or four students left over. They were never the same ones, because of me controlling the choice of captains.

For judging, we used a logical rubric:1. practiced seriously as a group, 2. spoke up and with expression, 3. came in on cue, and 4. kept the pace going.

Practicing consisted of the three groups who got their characters sorted, helped each other pronounce words and practiced at the same time, while the judges walked from group-to-group judging.

After a practice period, each group presented the same play to all of us. The length of the practice period was subjective. It depended on the "mood' of the class that day.

The judges got together with me and chose a winner. We were never in disagreement, and we never had a tie. We also told the winners what they did well, based on the rubric.

We had block scheduling so there was time to include the play as one of our activities for the class.

Teacher and judges selected a winner based on focused team practice, how well the audience could hear them, if they knew lines and were not lost and spoke with emphasis.

Oral Book Report.

Do not use a hatchet to remove a fly from your Friend's forehead.
(Chinese Proverb)

Every week students were required to present an oral book report to the class. That meant taking students who don't like to read to the library, searching for a book, keeping the book in their backpack for the week and presenting their report week after week.

"Surely you jest," you may think; but it was true, and I say "Yes, it is possible."

The plan went like this. I took each of my reading classes to the library. The librarian pretended to be glad to see us. I would stay with my students while they roamed the non-fiction section, instead of the usual, "May I help you find a book?" because no one wanted a book. Most believed the library was a dead zone to them. Actually, during one of the early visits, I heard a student say, "I've never been in a library." I would spend my time going from student to student asking what they found and where they found it. This line of questioning was heard by the other students and the buzz would begin. I would say so and so found a skateboarding book over there.

Mostly, they picked books that were thin, had a bright cover and lots of pictures with little reading required.

When they had checked out their book, they would sit at the long table. Some looked at their chosen book and some showed others, but mostly they would socialize with each other at a reduced volume. I would go back and forth between the sitting group and the students who were still searching.

As these trips to the library progressed, the students would make their own discoveries. I remember fondly, a moment when a girl found 'Chicken Soup for the Soul' and spread the word. The inspirational section had more business the next week. Another time, a student found 'Yucky Things'. It was full of grossness done in colorful pictures and great humor - perfect for young adolescents who don't like to read.

One time with a younger group somewhere else, a girl checked out a book written in French. She was a weak reader and believed I would not let her check it out of the library. I wondered why it was even there. She and her friend had a great time reading the book together all week. I never eavesdropped on their reading of the book in French, but I did envy their enjoyment.

The dreaded part was having to stand up in front of the class and give their report. The front of the room was always called the stage. In the big picture, I was interested in developing the habit of going to the library, enriching a sense of discovery, giving the library a positive spin and standing in front of the class 'on the stage' with a prepared report. The report consisted of 5 things: Have the copy with you so the class can see it, read out the title, copyright, where it was found in the library and whether they recommended it or not.

The student could write it out and read it or take the list with him and refer to it. As time went on, the students simply stood up on stage and told the class about the book. Being prepared became a non-issue.

Over time, I noticed more books were recommended than not. One reason was peer pressure. Students would make comments such as, "Why do you keep picking boring books?"

Politics at Titusville High

Great minds have always violent opposition from mediocre minds.
(Unknown)

Unfortunately, Dr Christy was promoted to the county office while I was teaching at THS. I, on the other hand, was left with Mark R, the new principal. At the first faculty meeting he directed his reading questions and concerns to the new first year English teacher right out of college. Talk about feedback to me. From then on, I was out of the reading curriculum - even though I was the reading teacher.

How did I get on the "out team" after two years on the "in team?" The only thing that came to mind was I told him to listen to the older teachers and I was one of the old ones; but I had not been there for years as most of the others - I didn't mean that kind of old. I meant the established teachers who were caring for the school culture while principals came and went. One fourth of all teachers at Titusville High were former alumni of the school.

The assistant principal would now enter my room to take away the earphones that the students were using with the book on tape program. I was the last one to be evaluated on the last day to evaluate. It was another big clue that politics was afoot. I received two 'needs improvement', which meant I could be transferred to another school or let go because I did not have three years at the school. I was closing in on my third year at the school when this happened. I would have had continued contract status if I had finished the year but not with two 'needs improvement'. The writing was on the wall. Two 'needs improvement' meant I should move on, so I accepted a position at Mims Elementary school for the last quarter of the current year.

Fortunately, I put myself and my bike down on the pavement on my ride home to avoid an accident with a car. I avoided the accident but unfortunately, I popped my shin bone through my skin, so I had to go out on disability and had no job for the next year. Back to my planning board.

Unfortunately, the first year English teacher, who also got teacher of the year, went out for the rest of the year after having a breakdown. Mark R. unknowingly burned his bridges with Brevard County and was not re-hired.

Lucky Break

*You are the only problem you will ever have and you are the only answer. **(Unknown)***

While I was recovering from my busted-up ankle - two titanium plates and nine screws - I wrote software programs to teach the vocabulary of the state standardized Florida Testing (FCAT).

Fortunately, the new principal at Glendridge, Vertis Lane, heard about the logic of my software program and tried it out at her school. She agreed with me that the students needed to understand the vocabulary of the test and how to find the correct answer. The first teacher to use the program, used the computer program as the teacher. She spent her time in class working on her part-time job with Pampered Chef. I was called in to show her how she was to interact with the class using the software program and not simply run the software.

The program was in three parts: Firstly, was learning the terms the students would encounter while reading the test, such as, 'main idea'.

The second part was to practice where to look for the answer. The third part was to demonstrate mastery in small teacher-led groups of three or four students while the rest of the class continued to work with the software on their computers.

In the small groups, students would explain the terms in the directions, practice where to find the correct answer and recognize the correct answer among similar choices.

Three teachers used the Read 180 program while one teacher used the software from my company, Garland Institute.

The state of Florida requires that in order to show achievement, at least 50 % of students must reach level 3 or above. The Garland Institute program had 51 % of students reach level 3 or above; which was a 17% increase over the previous year. The Read 180 program yielded a 3% increase with just 5% of the students reaching the state required achievement.

Unfortunately, Vertis, the principal at Glendridge Middle, took a position at the county office and I sucked at marketing it, so I only made the one sale.

Chapter 14

Map Drawing

Quality is never an accident.
It is always the result of high intention,
sincere effort, intelligent direction
and skillful execution.
It represents the wiser
of many alternatives.
(Will A. Faster)

My last teaching assignment was in the Alternative School. I needed a new challenge. I was looking for the students who fell through the gaping cracks in education. I wanted to see how they were doing and if I could help them get back to a regular class with a bag of new positive habits. In a U.S. history class, I had students draw a map of the U S A. I explained over the groans and chatter about the task being impossible that it was not for a grade. We held the maps up and laughed all round. There was a small amount of trepidation by some to having their ignorance exposed, but I had the most out-going student start and they blazed the trail.

I am sure you are wondering how I got a group of high school students in the Alternative School to draw a map of the USA in colored pencils and crayons on large white drawing paper.

I had the students draw a map of the USA on scrap paper and among the groans, I expressed my certainty that they would not be good that we would all admire the effort and enjoy the laughter. Yes, we all had a good laugh at our first attempts.

We spent a lot of time in the New England colonies and a couple of minutes on the West coast. I was pretty sure I should not bring in the tempera paint for this project. There wasn't any to be had, anyway. I was lucky to have enough books of one kind for a whole class.

I promised them they would pull it off and I was so confident that I was going to post their drawings in the hall. By now many were groaning, but with a smile on their faces. Well, maybe a couple showed disbelief. It was so 'elementary' but I had done a lot of 'tongue in cheek' with them by now, so they were not put off by having their map in the hall.

In my mind, I told myself there was at least one student who secretly always wanted his/her work displayed in a class - any class - let alone the hall. Way back in their mind, I am sure the students believed it would be a good one by the time their map made it to the hall.

The second step was to practice. For part of each class, we practiced drawing the outline of New England. Then each state had to be drawn in and labeled with the correct abbreviation.

Students would practice using our abundant supply of scrap paper. (I had found piles of ditto sheets from the previous teacher.) When the student was ready to be checked out, he/she would close the book and draw from memory and bring it to me.

Step three was the time for me to make a public announcement of my comments such as, "Oh, so close, only off by one." "You got it last time, but you missed it this time", "You missed the same one again". "Try this memory trick."

Step three was drawing New England on the special large white drawing paper. There was peer pressure to catch the leader. The large pieces of white paper containing the maps in progress were kept in a special place in the class out of harms' way. Only Mrs. Atwood could pass out the paper and collect the maps.

As we progressed through the curriculum, we applied the same model to learning the rest of the states. In general, my students quickened the process, and we did get our maps in the hall. No one defaced them or made fun of them. My best map drawer got expelled from Alternative School, but I put his map up in the hall, too. Rachel didn't get to finish hers, but we put it up with the finished maps. She never had a chance. She died from an overdose one Friday night after school.

Create a Civilization and Then Have it Collapse

*Knowledge becomes wisdom only after it has been put to practical use. (**Unknown**)*

While teaching world history at the Alternative School in Titusville, Fl, I had my high school world history class create a great civilization and then destroy it.

I am sure you are wondering how to get students in the Alternative School to come up with a successful rich civilization, write about its greatness and then have it destroyed by some catastrophic event. That is a lot of writing and research.

What's the catch, you ask? It seemed quite an abstract concept. What am I glossing over? This is what was revealed to me by the students.

Firstly, we decided how to present the project. No paragraphs were expected, but lists were fine - even no lists and just pictures were fine, too. With the simple format decided, we agreed on what was common to all the great civilizations that we were learning about. As a group, they listed characteristics of the great civilizations that were established. Each student now knew what to write about and everyone wrote full sentences.

The questioning procedure was part of the magic that made the project work. For example: "What do you need every day to survive"? At this point the discussion becomes a brainstorming session. All answers were accepted. When the students got closer to the answer, I was modelling a form of Socratic questioning, which turned into a version of charades or even the childhood game of 'Hot, hot, boiling and cold, cold, freezing'. At this level of questioning everyone was awake and adding to the discussion. The answers were silly, funny, insightful, lively and enlightening about how students' minds work with association memory.

The second step was what I call 'one-on-one' with each student. I became a consultant commenting on clever ideas and when a student got stuck, I gave several suggestions and let the student pick his/her favorite option. All students could listen to my consultations and borrow ideas. Sometimes a student would come up with an option that another student used.

Collapsing civilization was a fun brainstorming event, too. There was war, illness (such as the plague), cataclysmic events, resources drying up, etc.

All the students' papers were displayed on the wall in the hall. It was so elementary, but I was quite proud to have made it work.

Fake it Until You Make It.

*Feel the fear and do it anyway. **(Unknown)***

My last teaching assignment was teaching grades 6 – 12 Reading at the Alternative School. I gave each new student a list of rules titled 'How to be a Student'. I call these rules: Fake it Until You Make It.

1. Number one is staring at some part of the teacher's face when the teacher speaks. The teacher will think you are interested.

2. Another one is lean forward when the teacher speaks. The teacher will think you are more interested.

3. Stay in your assigned seat and do not get up without permission. Your parents expect me to keep you safe, daily in my class.

4. Raise your hand at least three times in each class even if you do not know the answer. Your raised hand shows you are interested. If the teacher does call on you and you do not know the answer, ask to have the question repeated. You can also say you just forgot what you wanted to say.

5. Next on the list was, "Your beliefs control your attitude. Your attitude dictates your emotions. Your emotions control your actions. I can control my intentions, but I cannot control your perceptions. (unknown)

6. It is alright to make a mistake in the classroom, but more to your credit to make a different one each time. "We are what we

repeatedly do. Excellence, therefore, is not an act but a habit." (Aristotle)

Oh, the irony! When two students get expelled for fighting from the same grade level in regular school, both end up in the same class at the Alternative School. All fighters went back to being friends before they returned to regular school.

Why didn't the school just have them make up and go back to being friends at school? Zero tolerance for fighting does not ever allow for exceptions to the rule. There is always an exception to every rule and rules are abused before used.

Politics at the Alternative School

*I'm a joker who has understood his epoch and has extracted all he possibly could from the stupidity, greed and vanity of his contemporaries. (**Pablo Picasso**)*

I wanted to teach at the Alternative School. I interviewed and accepted the position. Bill, the principal, introduced me to the staff and said, "I asked her what she did with Keagen because he had a 'B' in her class at Madison, his regular school."

She said to me, "I made him work."

He said "I am expecting great things from her. She has lots of experience."

From my experience, we do a disservice to the students at the Alternative School if we do not make effective change. To make effective change, the laws of physics need to be applied. For every action there is an equal and opposite reaction.

In the classroom we call this Law of Physics Consequences, positive and negative. Consequences only work if the variable consistency is applied every day and in every instance. The action is called feedback. Think of the coaching metaphor. It is all about feedback move by move, event by event, practice by practice. Everything we say to students should be about feedback which needs to become a constant flow that is informal, verbal and written, as in a grade; and formally, such as a detention or referral.

Build the feedback system with the end in mind. The product in our schools is the Florida Curriculum Assessment Test. (FCAT) The path becomes clear, the variables can be defined: motivation, attitude, goal, challenge, reality check, skills, self-evaluation, stamina, internalized practice.

The ultimate practice must be between the student and the questions. The guess option must be relegated from first choice to a very last resort. Students must move through the process of building a system for taking the FCAT. I find students are usually at point A - reads the story, reads the question, reads the choices and then guesses at the answer and moves on. The goal is to finish and the quicker the better. I end with students who look over everything before beginning, choose from their bag of tricks for figuring out meaning, find the answer in the material and save guessing as a last resort when the choice is between two answers only. The countless practice sessions with immediate teacher feedback builds confidence that a 5 is possible on the FCAT.

The research provides the road map through the process. First and foremost, the best brain research says to get the brain's attention.

Through the research we know that the brain loves the smell of peppermint, lemon and cinnamon, so give each student a peppermint to smell or eat at the beginning of each class. Mr. D., you took that away. You said there was one smashed on the floor and that some student had peppermints in a pencil case and one smashed on the computer keyboard. This was reported to me after peppermints had been used in my class for a year and a half. Your response was no more peppermints. Brain candy denied.

Again, the research says to get the brain's attention, provide something unexpected. The brain loves a paradox. What better way than through pictured beauty, sense of wonder, disbelief or even pearls of laughter.

When the students enter the room they become students, the brain is turned on with peppermint and delighted to focus on the white board projections of pictures or short video clips. Mr. D., you took that away from my students. Many of the students had never experienced some of the sights or new inventions or nature's beauty. You said it was not relevant to the subject. I had been using this research for a year and half at school. Your response was no more video clips from the internet. "Eye candy" denied.

A wonderful way to open the brain is through music. At 60 beats per minute, it can produce alpha waves conducive to relaxation and learning. Pachelbel Canon in D major is playing when students enter the room and during silent reading. That part of the research you allowed. The brain also uses music to concentrate. The music blocks out extraneous background noise. Students used the computers to provide a background of music while they worked. Mr. D, you said it was wrong to allow students to listen to music while they work. You said that they could be listening to inappropriate music. You did not want the students on Grooveshark site last year and this information is posted at each machine. You took away research-based learning with music even though no one in the class could hear appropriate or inappropriate music because the students wore earphones. Music denied.

At the beginning of the year, Mrs. Sparks, principal at Madison Middle, complimented me on my FCAT scores. Thirty of my students scored a 5, the highest score on the reading section. I was not teaching reading. I was teaching social studies, and I taught how to read a question and find the correct answer. My FCAT scores were outstanding. My process of learning finds specific ways to engage their brains, understand the question asked and where to find the answer.

The culture of the classroom is developed through the laws of physics. Given to us to use are detentions and referrals. Students know it is okay to make a mistake in my class, but it is better to make a different mistake each time. Students have learned my line is always drawn and the consequences known and expected, if not always appreciated now. Profanity is one rule on which you drew the line. You said you may be old-fashioned but expected us not to allow profanity. Not only did I agree but I wrote students a referral which meant a trip to the principal's office for profanity and no, I never had the need to use profanity myself in class.

Because of all the changes you made in the ways in which I could teach, the reprimands that you have given me for disciplining students, and the total lack of respect that you have shown for the way I teach and try to reach students, I am no longer able to give detentions or referrals for profanity.

At this point, the students know that they have been released by you to wreak havoc in my classroom. I now have students who have stopped working and are using profanity, saying "D. won't do anything to us". I even had a student stand up and practice slapping his balls against his skin somewhere in his pants to make a smacking sound. He called it tea bagging.

Who controls the window analogy? If the window is closed, you do not control the window. If the window is closed, the student controls the window. When the window is half open the teacher and the student share the window. This means neither the teacher nor the student controls the window. There is no control between the teacher and student. You and the student are on the same page. Remember the mule story. You have the student's attention. Learning can take place. It is called a 'teachable moment'.

In my situation, the windows of the recently added students became closed. The students controlled the window. The students were given permission to close the window on the teacher. Instead of the 'teachable' window, half open, half closed, I had students enjoying the power Mr. D. gave the new arrivals.

At that point, I had only one choice which was to take a leave of absence. Later, you tried to get me to retrieve my personal possessions from the classroom so they would not get lost, but you wanted me in your office to complete my yearly review. It would have been a nasty set up by you, so I happily went to Saint Croix and house-sat for my old college friend. I had no time for your surprise attack. I was enjoying my view of the aqua blue of the Caribbean from my house and pool on the mountainside.

Chapter 15

Great Teachers

Whomever is not a cynic at forty, can never have loved mankind (Unknown)

What do great teachers have in common? Connie Muther observed and interviewed more than sixty teachers who were highly valued by their colleagues and students. She found the teachers shared three qualities. Firstly, they love teaching, the content they are teaching and their students. Probably no one would dispute these three qualities, but there is more. The second is that these outstanding teachers bring their personal experiences, hobbies and interests into their teaching. In her words, she said the more wonderful the teacher, the weirder they are. Thirdly, great teachers have a mission or passion. For many of them, their passion comes from pain: they want to protect students from the pain they themselves suffered. As a group, great teachers dislike colleagues who complain, especially about students, and they regret not being able to share their ideas more with their peers. Advice from this group of teachers to educators, Muther added, boils down to this: "If you don't love kids, get out."

Do not erase the designs the child makes in the soft wax of his inner life. (Montessori)

Do not offer the child the content of the mind, but the order for that content. (Montessori)

The teacher's first duty is to watch over the environment, and this takes precedence over all the rest. Its influence is indirect, but unless it be well done there will be no effective and permanent results of any kind, physical, intellectual or spiritual. (Montessori)

The teacher, when she begins work in our schools, must have a kind of faith that the child will reveal himself through work. (Montessori)

Great tact and delicacy are necessary for the care of the mind of a child from three to six years, and an adult can have very little of it. (Montessori)

Education demands, then, only this: the utilization of the inner powers of the child for his own instruction. (Montessori)

The teacher must derive not only the capacity, but the desire, to observe natural phenomena. The teacher must understand and feel her position of observer: the activity must lie in the phenomenon. (Montessori)

In the psychological realm of relationship between teacher and child, the teacher's part and its techniques are analogous to those of the valet; they are to serve, and to serve well: to serve the spirit. (Montessori)

Your Line is Always Drawn

It's not so much what is poured into a student but what is planted that really counts. (**Unknown**)

"Her line is always drawn." said by Eric, explaining my class rules to another student.

"You like everyone, but you like some more." said Sharon who was explaining to me that I did not have favorites at the expense of other students.

"You're the bomb!" said my obnoxious-acting black student back when Blacks were changing the meaning in some words to mean the opposite. It was a compliment when I thought about it.

"You look like my sister." "You look like my mother." "You look like my grandmother." said by students as I grew older.

"You are strict but fair." said many students over the years. I took it to mean I was consistent and being consistent should be your constant variable.

"You need to stay in your seat and pass the paper forward or you will make our row have to do it all over again." said my Bellwether students over the years.

"You're a nice teacher but you are boring every once in a while. Have a nice summer." said my student, Billy.

"You were very nice and strict, too. Keep up the good work and have a good life." said Stephen.

"Mrs. Atwood, well, this year has been fun! At the beginning it was rough, but it turned out to be a good year! Thanks for no homework and have a good summer." said Brooke. "PS The labs were funnn!!!"

"You have been a good and great teacher. You've helped me a lot, especially with my attitude in class." said Michelle.

"You are the best English teacher I ever had. You are a nice person and you listened to what I had to say and I thank you for that." said Dan.

"There's going to be a lot of bad times, but you can make it; so hope you will always be a nice teacher and when you ever need me, I'll be in your heart, I hope." John Michael.

"Well, it was a OK year. We had our ups and downs. You sometimes acted like a witch and me too, so I hope you have a nice summer." said Ramone, my number one student.

"You let me work at my own pace and I really appreciate that." said Kathi.

"I really respect you for continuously pushing people to work. That teaches responsibility." said Steve.

"I will try to start keeping my mouth shut in class from now on. I learned a lot in here. I can't believe I am so smart." said Jennifer.

"For some odd reason, you're my favorite teacher Ha! Ha!" said Kellee.

"We had some pretty rough times, but everything seemed to work itself out. Thanks for the laughs." said Christopher.

"I thought every teacher on earth was a problem. You proved me wrong. I may not see you again but from now on, I will make passing grades in English." said Rusty.

"You know, I didn't think teachers had a heart, but I have changed my insight about teachers. It is like I have known you forever and I am not going to let you down. I'm gonna go in that class and pay attention to what that teacher has to say and I'm gonna ace that class. When I find myself messing up, I'm gonna look and say I wouldn't wanna let you down." said Tracy.

"Mrs. Atwood you are one of the meanest teachers I've ever had, but I think you set me straight." said Jared.

"Well, you taught me to have a sense of humor." said Fred.

"I also enjoyed watching you balance discipline and order with patience. It has been amusing at times to say the least." said A.K.A. Andy

Chapter 16

Symphony

**"If this little world tonight
Suddenly should fall through space In an instant every trace
Of the little crawling things
Ants, philosophers, and lice,
Cattle, cockroaches, and kings,
Beggars, millionaires, and mice,
Men and maggots all as one-on-one
As it falls into the sun...
It's hissing, headlong flight,
Shriveling from off its face
As it falls into the sun,
Who can say but at the same
Instant from some planet far
A child may watch us and exclaim:
"See the pretty shooting star."
(Oliver Herford)**

The best analogy for teaching is conducting a symphony. It is a lot of work. You have to write the music for each instrument. Sometimes you have to invent the instrument with your student. You have to teach each student how to play his/her instrument. You must develop acceptable music from each student. You must teach students that each is part of the whole. And practice, practice, practice.

Enjoy those moments when you achieve synergy and pedagogy. It was for those days that I taught